THE
Middlesteins

Center Point
Large Print

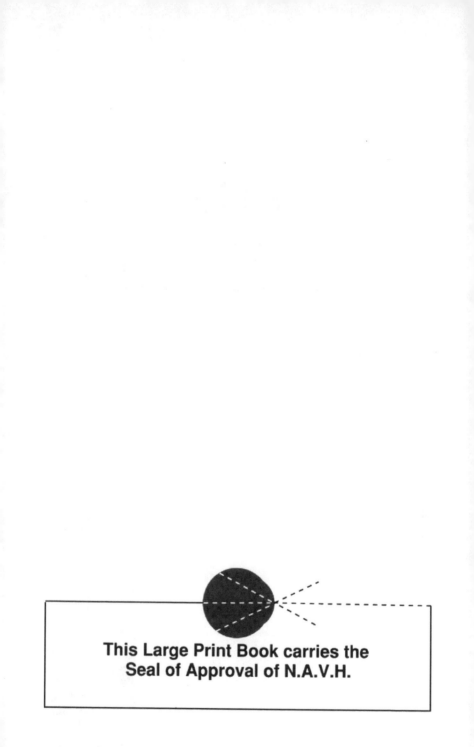

**This Large Print Book carries the
Seal of Approval of N.A.V.H.**

THE
Middlesteins

JAMI ATTENBERG

CENTER POINT LARGE PRINT
THORNDIKE, MAINE

This Center Point Large Print edition
is published in the year 2013 by arrangement with
Grand Central Publishing,
a division of Hachette Book Group, Inc.

This book is a work of fiction.
Names, characters, places, and incidents are
the product of the author's imagination or are used
fictitiously. Any resemblance to actual events, locales,
or persons, living or dead, is coincidental.

The text of this Large Print edition is unabridged.
In other aspects, this book may vary
from the original edition.
Printed in the United States of America
on permanent paper.
Set in 16-point Times New Roman type.

ISBN: 978-1-61173-624-3

Library of Congress Cataloging-in-Publication Data

Attenberg, Jami.
The Middlesteins / Jami Attenberg.
pages ; cm.
ISBN 978-1-61173-624-3 (library binding : alk. paper)
1. Families—Fiction. 2. Life change events—Fiction.
   3. Middle West—Fiction. 4. Large type books. I. Title.
PS3601.T784M53 2013
813′.6—dc23

2012037120

FOR MY FAMILY

THE
Middlesteins

Edie, 62 Pounds

HOW COULD SHE not feed their daughter?

Little Edie Herzen, age five: not so little. Her mother had noticed this, how could she miss it? Her arms and legs, once peachy and soft, had blossomed into something that surpassed luscious. They were disarmingly solid. A child should be squeezable. She was a cement block of flesh. She breathed too heavy, like someone's gassy old uncle after a meal. She hated taking the stairs; she begged to be carried up the four flights to their apartment, her mother *uchhing,* her back, the groceries, a bag of books from the library.

"I'm tired," said Edie.

"We're all tired," said her mother. "Come on, help me out here." She handed Edie the bag of books. "You picked these out, you carry them."

Her mother, not so thin herself. Nearly six feet tall, with a powerhouse of a body, she was a lioness who had a shimmer and a roar to her thick, majestic self. She believed she was a queen among women. Still, she was damp, and she had a headache, and the stairs weren't fun, she agreed.

Her husband, Edie's father, always took the stairs two at once, in a hurry to get to the next place. He was tall, with a thick head of dark, spongy hair, and had long, lanky, pale limbs, and his chest was so thin it was practically translucent, his ribs protruding, watery blue veins threaded throughout. After they made love, she would lazily watch the skin that covered his heart bob up and down, fast, slower, slow.

At meals, he ate and ate; he was carnal, primal, about food. He staked out territory, leaning forward on the table, one arm resting around his plate, the other dishing the food into his mouth, not stopping to chew or breathe. But he never gained a pound. He had starved on his long journey from Ukraine to Chicago eight years before, and had never been able to fill himself up since.

When you looked at all the things in the world there were to agree upon, they had so little in common, this husband and wife. He was not a patriot; America had always been her home. She was more frivolous than he with money, because to her, living in this vast, rich country, in the healthy city of Chicago, it always felt as if more money could be made. They went to separate synagogues, he to the one favored by the Russian immigrants, she to the one founded by Germans two generations earlier, where her parents had gone before they had died, the synagogue in which she had grown up, and she could not let that go, not even in this new union. He had more secrets, had seen more hardships. She had only watched it on the news. And he would always carry his daughter, Edie, wherever she wanted to go, on his shoulders, high up in the sky, as close to God as he could get her. And she was absolutely certain that Edie should be walking everywhere by now.

But they agreed about how to have sex with each other (any way they wanted, no judgment allowed) and how often (nightly, at least), and they agreed that food was made of love, and was what made love, and they could never deny themselves a bite of anything they desired.

And if Edie, their beloved, big-eyed, already sharp-witted daughter, was big for her age, it did not matter.

Because how could they not feed her?

Little Edie Herzen, having a bad day, was making the slowest walk up a flight of stairs in the collective history of walking and stairs, until she decided she could not take another step. It was hot in the stairwell, the dusty air overheated by a skylight above, and when Edie finally sat, throwing the bag of books on the floor next to her, the sweat squished down the backs of her thighs onto the stairs.

"Edie, *bubbeleh*, don't start."

"It's too hot," she said. "Hot, tired. Carry me."

"With what hands?"

"Where's Daddy? He could carry me."

"What is wrong with you today?"

Edie didn't mean to be a baby about it. She was not a whiner. She just wanted to be carried. She wanted to be carried and cuddled and fed salty liverwurst and red onion on warm rye bread. She wanted to read and talk and laugh and watch television and listen to the radio, and at the end of the day she wanted to be tucked into bed, and kissed good night by one or both of her parents, it did not matter which, for she loved them both equally. She wanted to watch the world around her go by, and make up stories in her head about everything she saw, and sing all the little songs they taught her in Sunday school, and count as high as she could possibly count, which was currently over one thousand. There was so much to be observed and considered, why did she need to walk? She missed her buggy and sometimes would pull it out of the storage closet and study it wistfully. She would have loved to be pushed around forever, like a princess in a carriage, surveying her kingdom, preferably one with a magical forest, with tiny dancing elves in it. Elves who had their own deli where they only sold liverwurst.

Her mother shifted the groceries in her damp arms. She could smell something sour and realized it was herself, and then a massive rivulet of sweat shot from her armpit down her arm, and she tried to wipe her arm against the bag, and then the bag began to turn, and she reached out for it with the other arm, and then the other bag began to fall, and she hunched over and held them close, trying to rest the bags on the tops of her thighs, but it did not matter, the groceries at the top of both bags spilled out: first the loaf of bread, the greens, the tomatoes, landing on Edie's head, and then two large cans of beans on Edie's fingertips.

Little Edie Herzen, lioness in training, already knew how to roar.

Her mother dropped the bags to the floor. She grabbed her daughter, she held her against her, she squeezed her (wondering again why Edie was already so solid, so *hard*), she shushed her baby girl, the guilt boiling in her stomach like an egg in hot water, a lurching sensation between wanting her daughter to stop crying already—she was going to be fine in five minutes, five years, fifty years, she would not even remember this pain— and wanting to cry herself, because she knew she would never forget the time she dropped two cans of beans on her daughter's fingers.

"Let me see them," she said to Edie, who was howling and shaking her head at the same time, holding her hands tight against her. "We won't know if you're all right if I can't look at them."

The howling and the hiding of the hands went on for a while. Neighbors opened their doors and stuck their heads into the hallway, then closed them when they saw it was just that fat child from 6D, being a kid, crying like they do. Edie's mother coddled and begged. The ice cream was melting. One nail was going to turn blue and fall off a week later, and if she thought Edie was hollering now, she hadn't heard anything, but no one knew that yet. There would be no scars, although there would be a lifetime of scars ahead for Edie, in one way or another, but no one knew that yet either.

Her mother sat there with her arm around her daughter, until she did the only thing left she could do. She reached behind them on the floor and grabbed the loaf of rye bread, still warm in its wrapping paper, baked not an hour before at Schiller's down on Fifty-third Street, and pulled off a hunk of it and handed it to her daughter, who ignored her, and continued to sob, unforgiving, a tiny mean bone having just been formed.

"Good," said her mother. "More for me."

How long do you think it took before Edie turned her head and stuck her trembling hand out for food? Her mouth hanging open expectantly, yet drowsily, like a newborn bird. Rye to her mouth. Wishing there were liverwurst. Dreaming of elves. How long until she revealed her other hand, pink, and purple, and blue, the edges of her index finger's nail bloodied, to her mother? Until her mother covered her hand with kisses? Food was made of love, and love was made of food, and if it could stop a child from crying, then there was nothing wrong with that either.

"Carry me," Edie said, and this time her mother

could no longer deny her. Up the stairs, four flights, the bag of library books strapped around her neck, only slightly choking her, while one arm held two bags of groceries, and the other held her beloved daughter, Edie.

The Meanest Act

ROBIN'S MOTHER, EDIE, was having another surgery in a week. Same procedure, different leg. Everyone kept saying, *At least we know what to expect.* Robin and her downstairs neighbor, Daniel, were toasting the leg at the bar across the street from their apartment building. It was cold out. January in Chicago. Robin had worn five layers just to walk across the street. Daniel was already drunk by the time she got there. Her mother was getting cut open twice in one year. Cheers.

The bar was a no-name, no-shame, no-nothing kind of place. Robin had a hard time giving directions to it. There was a fluorescent Old Style sign in the sole window, but no number on the front door. *Between 242 and 246* is what she would say, although for some reason that confused people. But not Daniel. He knew the way.

"Here's to number two," said Daniel. He raised his glass. He was drinking the brown stuff. Usually he drank the yellow stuff or the amber stuff, but it was winter. "Is it the right or the left leg?"

"You know, I can't even remember. I think I've blocked it out. Isn't that terrible? Am I a terrible person?" All of it had been a surprise, though it shouldn't have been. Her mother refused to eat properly or exercise, and in the last decade she had grown obese. Two years ago, she had been diagnosed with diabetes. It was an advanced case. The diabetes, combined with a disastrous gene pool, had led to an arterial disease in her legs. What had started out as tingling had turned to constant pain. Robin had seen her mother's legs in the hospital, after the first surgery, and had gagged at their blue tinge. How had her mother not noticed? Or her father? How had this slipped through the cracks? The doctor had inserted a small metal tube—a stent—into her leg, so that the blood could flow properly. (Robin wondered: where did the blood go, if it did not flow?) Originally the doctor had wanted to do a bypass, an idea that threatened everyone. He still did, according to Robin's brother, Benny. "This could get serious fast," he had told her. "We've been warned." But Edie had negotiated with the doctor. She promised to behave herself. She promised to do the work to get herself right. Thirty-five years as a lawyer, she knew how to put up a fight. Six months later Edie had changed nothing in her life, taken not one step to help herself, and here they all were again.

"It's not that I don't care," said Robin. "It's just that I don't want to know." She knew too much already. This was real life, kicking her in the face, and she wanted nothing to do with it.

Last weekend she had gone home to check on the madness, back to the suburb where she had grown up and then evacuated thirteen years earlier, hoping never to return, but finding herself there all too much these days. Her mother had picked her up in front of the train station, and then driven around the corner and parked in front of a movie theater. It was late afternoon; there had been a half day at the school where Robin taught. (She'd had fantasies about what she would do with that free afternoon: a long run along the lake during the warmest part of the day, or an early bender with Daniel. But it was not to be.) Senior citizens walked out of the matinee as if in slow motion. A few stay-at-home moms dragged their toddlers toward the parking lot across the street. Robin almost hurled herself out of the car after them. *Take me with you.*

"There's something I need to tell you before we go home," her mother had said, heavy breath, hulking beneath her fur coat, no flesh visible except for her putty-colored face, her drooping chin, her thick-ringed neck. "Your father has left me. He's had enough."

"This is a joke," said Robin.

"This is for real," said her mother. "He's flown the coop, and he's not coming back."

What a weird way to put it, Robin realized later. As if her father were being held like some house pet, trapped in a cage lined with shit-stained

19

newspaper. Her feelings for her father swerved wildly in that moment. Her mother was tough. The situation was tough. He had taken the coward's way out, but Robin had never begrudged people their cowardice; it was simply a choice to be made. Still, she hated herself for thinking like that. This was her mother, and she was sick, and she needed help. Thrown up against her admittedly fragile moral code, Robin knew that there was an obvious judgment to be made. His decision was despicable. Her train of thought would never be uttered out loud, only the final resolution: Her father would not be forgiven. She had not liked him much before this happened, though she had loved him, and it did not take much to push her over the edge toward something close to hatred, or at the least the dissolution of love.

Her mother was sobbing. She touched her mother's hand. She put her hand on her mother's shoulder. Edie was shaking, and her lips were blue. One step from death, thought Robin. But she was no doctor.

"I should have treated him better," said her mother.

Robin could not argue with her, but still, all she could do was blame her father. Richard Middlestein had signed up for a life with Edie Herzen. And Edie was still alive.

And so the surgery had seemed irrelevant at the time. Robin hadn't even bothered to ask her about her health. Her brother was taking care of all that most of the time anyway. Robin had gone to the first surgery, sat there for a few hours in the waiting room like everyone else—*Boring;* they all knew she was going to be fine, it was a simple procedure, and she'd be out of the hospital that night—and then had claimed she was too busy for the next one. Robin had thought she'd gotten off scot-free, even if it meant she was a horrible human being. Her reliable, solid, family-focused brother, Benny, who lived two towns away from her parents, would be there. Him, his wife with the nose job, her niece and nephew, Emily and Josh, all of them patiently waiting alongside her father for her mother to surface. How many worried children was it going to take to screw in that lightbulb anyway?

But this latest trauma was something new and unusual. This was heartbreak. And abandonment. And Benny was not even remotely prepared to deal with anything like that. Robin's mind traveled to other people in her mother's life who might be able to help her, like her longtime friends from the synagogue, the Cohns and the Grodsteins and the Weinmans and the Frankens. Forty years they'd known each other. But they were all still married, and they knew nothing of this business. No, this was Robin's territory. Always single, probably for a reason. At last she had been called up to bat.

"You are definitely not a terrible person," said Daniel. He scratched his soft-looking blond beard. Robin had been imagining for months that it was soft. Everything about him looked soft and comforting, but also mildly weak, as well. His beard and mustache and the hair on his head and the hair on his chest and belly—she had seen him sunning himself on his back porch on a number of occasions that past summer, sprawled out on a faded hammock—were all golden and feathery. She had even tried to pat him on the head once, just to see what his hair felt like, but he had taken the flight of her hand as the beginning of a high five and had raised his own hand to meet hers, and she had no choice but to respond.

Whatever, it was just hair. She didn't need to touch it. She had her own hair, which was plenty soft on its own, black, curly, long, springy, wiry, but still soft.

And anyway, then there was the rest of him, the belly bloated by the yellow-amber-brown stuff, slung low and wide over the belt of his pants, his own personal air bag; the droopy, faded flannel shirts, with the holes in the cuffs and the pockets; the white-blue jeans and corduroys with the frayed knees; the Converse high-tops with the tape around the bottoms to keep the soles on. The bloodshot eyes. The torn cuticles. The amount of time he spent online. (Sure, it was his job, but still it concerned her.) The only time he left the house was to go to this bar, or when Robin dragged him on walks in warmer weather.

"Your boyfriend Daniel," is what her roommate, Felicia, called him.

"He's not my boyfriend," she would say back.

"You sure act like it," Felicia would say. "What do you talk about on those walks of yours?"

They talked about her mother. Just like they were doing now.

"I don't know how to help her," she said.

"I think you just have to be there for her," he said.

She knew that was what she was supposed to do, but every time she took that train home, and the view slowly transformed from the high, gleaming architecture of downtown Chicago in the distance to the swirling mass of strip- and mini- and mall-malls that defined the burbs—there was more to the suburbs, she knew that, but that was all she could ever see anymore, her view obscured by a combination of prejudice and neurosis—a deep depression began to constrict her.

If she had never moved back to Chicago from New York, none of this would be happening. She knew it in her gut. She had lasted there only a year, one year with four other girls in a tired old floor-through in Bushwick, with a creaky ceiling and neighbors who seemed to be constantly cooking. (Clanking pans, nonstop sizzles; why were they always frying something?) There were two windows in the apartment, one that faced an empty lot next door, and the other, which faced the trash-infested alleyway in the back. There were bars on the windows. Inside was prison, but outside was worse. Men made nasty comments to her on the street. She got called "white girl" a lot, and she hated it, even though she could not argue that point. She kept searching for the charm in her neighborhood but was neither equipped nor informed. She spent much of her time that year on a train to somewhere else in the city, anywhere else but there.

Her roommates were all the same as Robin, more or less. Their names were Jennifer and Julie and Jordan; they were all Jewish, they all had gone to midwestern colleges, and they all had individual secret joint bank accounts with their mothers, who would put a little extra in there every once in a while, so that they could treat themselves to something nice. There was a fifth roommate, who slept in the living room on the couch when she wasn't sleeping at her girl-friend's house. She was a brisk girl from Alaska, Teresa, who had grown up in a town of drunks, fighting her way to the middle class while the rest of the roommates did nothing but hover there.

They all had been brought together by the Teach for America program, and then spread out in terrible high schools across Brooklyn. Not quaint Park Slope Brooklyn, where the pretty people with babies lived, but east of there, on the way to racetracks and airports; on the way, it sometimes felt, to nowhere at all. Robin had not been prepared for any of it. Not even after a lifetime of consuming mass culture that told her how messed up schools in impoverished urban areas could be. Not a film or a song or an episode of *Law & Order* or a class in college or an orientation program had prepared her for how much one year teaching in a school full of at-risk kids was going to suck. If she was seeking hope and inspiration, or if she was thinking she was going to provide it, she was in the wrong place. She was way out of her league. Everyone knew it. She had no poker face. All day long she *flinched*.

She would wake up every morning and wonder if she was doing more harm than good. She spent money out of her own pocket on paper and markers. She tried to innovate: She covered a large empty tin can (last night's diced tomatoes for the pasta sauce) with paper and named it the "Hear Me Can" and placed it in the front of the classroom. "When you feel like yelling or you're upset about something, just write it down and put it in there," she instructed the children. "And I promise you will be heard."

After class, she would read the notes. Sometimes it was easy-to-take information.

Someone stole my pencil.
I don't like tests.
They should have chicken nuggets every
*   day at lunch.*

But more often, the missives were hateful or sad.

My father called me a faggot last night.
It's too loud to sleep in my house.
I hate you I hate these words I hate everyone.

But that wasn't why she left town, at least not in her memory. There had been an actual, concrete turning point, which had happened near the end of the school year. For a week she and her roommates had woken up covered in bites, at first just a few, but then days later, their bodies, their bellies, their legs, their arms, were covered in red, stinging marks. There was no denying it. They had bedbugs. Teresa was the one who had finally recognized what the bites were and what would have to be done about it. They would have to wash all their clothes in hot water. An exterminator would have to be called. "And you can't do anything but trash those mattresses," she said. Who had suggested they burn them first? Was it Robin? Would her mind have gone to destruction so quickly? If she wasn't the one who said it, she was definitely the one who agreed to it right away.

In an instant, they were all up. They could not live with the bug-infested objects in their lives a moment longer. They kicked their mattresses down the steps. Teresa single-handedly carried the couch herself. They dragged each item through the empty lot, across the gravel, and then to the filthy alley behind their house. Robin ran to the corner deli and bought some lighter fluid. One of the girls had some matches. The other girls picked through the alley for more flammable items: old newspapers, a lampshade, a half dozen dirty pizza-delivery boxes. They all stood there and watched the flames burn the mattresses. Burn those fuckers right up. They all stood there, scratching themselves. Was this what they deserved? They had *taught for America*.

Robin examined her mottled arm and said, "Screw this. I'm moving home."

"Me too," said Julie.

"Me too," said Jennifer.

"Me too," said Jordan.

"Not me," said Teresa. "I'm moving in with my girlfriend. New York is awesome."

Now Robin lived with just two roommates (one who was never there because she stayed with her boyfriend most of the time in some sort of undercover, "let's not offend our Catholic parents even though we're in our late twenties and are clearly not virgins any longer" gesture, and the other who was always there because she had nowhere better to be, much like Robin) in a spacious apartment in Andersonville, just three train stops away from the private school where she had taught history for the last seven years. Her life in Chicago was better in all the ways she had wanted it to be at the time she moved, although she wondered sometimes if she had left too soon, because she knew that she would never go back. This was it, Chicago. The end of the line.

Because she had a heartsick mother to take care of now.

And where would she have gone anyway, these past few years? No matter where, she would be living the same life as she had in Chicago. Robin would get up in the morning, sip coffee, do a few stretches, run five miles, shower, moisturize, pluck a stray hair from her chin, put on too much eyeliner, and then, before she left, water some plants she cared little for but kept alive out of habit. Then she would take a train or a bus to a school near enough where she wouldn't spend her whole life commuting, but far enough that she felt grown up—real adults left their homes and went somewhere to work; this was a problem she had with Daniel and his life and taking him seriously—and while she traveled, she would read whatever post-seventies novel she had secured from the library, and she would smirk at the funny parts but never laugh out loud. At school she would teach a class about the Vietnam War and she would get a little political but nothing too outrageous (she was clearly sympathetic with the protesters, but still, *We should always support our troops*), then have lunch with the one good friend she had made there—whoever the other caustic young single woman was—and they would sit alone together in the cafeteria and make fun of everyone else, students and teachers alike, while always finding something nice to say about them all in the end. Later she would take the train home, perhaps go grocery shopping, buying environmentally sound and mostly vegetarian food items, which she would cook for herself, eat peacefully, reading her book as she ate, using her index finger to follow along, then greet her roommate with a bright smile as she came into the room but then look down again quickly as if she could not be distracted from that exact emotional moment in the book, which was not really a lie, but was also an excuse to be quiet a little longer, to enjoy one more moment in the day that was hers alone. Because later she would go to a bar, with a man or maybe she would meet a man there, and she would practice being a woman, feel some sort of power, suck just enough energy from the man sitting across from her that she would still feel whole and relevant and sexual, without actually having to do anything, simply show up and be there. No one got hurt. She had no interest in getting hurt ever again, or hurting anyone else ever again. It was only a little conversation. Innocent flirtation. Then she would drink what she needed to knock herself out for the night.

Robin could live in Denver or San Francisco or Atlanta or Austin, and it wouldn't matter. She would be doing the same thing wherever she lived. She would never set furniture on fire in an alley again.

She thought about what it felt like right at the end of her morning run. She always sprinted, and by the time she made it home she was out of breath, and she would hunch over, her hands on her knees, her skin stung with heat. That was her favorite part of the day. That minute she sprinted.

She bent over on her barstool. Her hair hung down the sides of her face. She waited for the blood to rush to her head. Daniel put his hand on the back of her neck. He did not ask her if she was okay. She liked Daniel. He knew when to keep quiet.

Finally she raised her head. It wasn't the same feeling as when she sprinted. There was no faking that feeling.

Daniel and Robin toasted once again, this time to her parents' marriage.

"Truly an inspiration to us all," said Daniel.

"That's mean," she said.

"Oh, the surgeries are fine, but the divorce is off-limits? I see you for who you really are now, Robin. A sentimental old fool."

She was not sentimental. But she had excess love in her heart now; she knew that was true. She had taken it back from her father. It had not disappeared. But it needed redirection. Robin looked at Daniel and had the meanest thought of her entire life. *He'll do.*

She leaned over the corner of the bar, the edge of it pressing against her gut, and gave Daniel an awkward but not entirely terrible kiss. She sat back down in her seat.

Daniel said nothing for a minute. His eyes were glassy, and he rubbed his lips together. "We should talk about this first," said Daniel.

"This is absolutely the thing we should not talk about," said Robin. "Do not talk, and do not think. Just do."

Together, silently, they left.

Edie, 202 Pounds

EVERYBODY WAS OBSESSED with Golda Meir in Edie Herzen's house. Her father, and all his buddies, some from the synagogue, some from the university, a few fresh from Russia whom Edie's father had adopted into his life because he was always adopting people, spent weekends hunched over the kitchen table talking about her, smoking cigarettes and drinking coffee, picking at the food in front of them, the plates of white-fish and herring, the bagels, the lox, the various spreads of sometimes indeterminate meat. Bright green pickles bursting with vinegar and salt. The cherry pastries covered with half-melted squiggles of frosting.

Her mother would be slicing tomatoes and onions near the kitchen sink, a cigarette in her mouth, too. She wore her hair high and fluffy and dyed black, and there was always a new gold bracelet dangling around her wrist. She cared less than Edie's father did about all this, and she almost never went to the synagogue except on High Holidays. When they moved to Skokie ten years before from Hyde Park, they left behind the synagogue that Edie's mother had grown up with, and suddenly practicing her faith became irrelevant without a personal sense of history attached to it. But she supported her husband and his friends—they could do all the praying on her behalf. She'd make sure they got fed. No one would leave her house hungry. Those poor, wifeless, childless, lonely men.

The men went from the table to the synagogue and back again, some of them sprawling at night on their living-room couch. Israel was about to get bombed from all sides, and everyone was convinced that if Golda were running the show, and not that weak, stuttering excuse for a man, Eshkol, this would have been taken care of months ago. Edie thought about that T. S. Eliot poem she had been studying in English class: *In the room the women come and go, talking of Michelangelo.* In her house, it was the men coming and going, and they were always talking about Meir.

Sometimes her parents argued about how much money they were donating to Israel.

Edie ate everything the men ate, more than the men ate. They smoked, she ate. They drank coffee, she drank Coca-Cola. At night she ate the leftovers. It didn't matter, there was always new food coming through the door. She ate on behalf of Golda, recovering from cancer. She ate in tribute to Israel. She ate because she loved to eat. She knew she loved to eat, that her heart and soul felt full when she felt full, and also because she had heard one of her father's older friends,

Abraham, speaking about her to Naumann, blue-eyed, watery-skinned, a drinker, only a few years older than she was, a young man in her house to look at and talk to up close and personal if she chose, which she had not.

"Big-boned, my ass. That girl just loves to eat," is what Abraham said.

So what? That's what she had to say about that. Even if it had hurt a little bit to hear him say those words, it meant that they were still looking at her.

As a much younger man, Abraham had escaped serving in the Russian army during the war with Japan by puncturing both of his eardrums. He had worn hearing aids since. All her father's friends respected him for his subversive behavior, because they all hated Russia (and sometimes America) (but loved Israel) but Edie thought that was the act of an insane man. For the rest of your life to be deaf? She could stop eating (maybe), but he'd never get his hearing back.

Naumann's father had known Edie's father when they were children in Kiev. They had not been close, but her father had a hard time saying no to any of the pleading letters that came his way. Naumann had been staying on the living-room couch off and on for a few months. It was covered in plastic, and she had no idea how he slept on it without sliding off. Abraham would pass out upright on the recliner in the basement. Edie's mother would cover them both with blankets that were always neatly folded in the morning when Edie would stumble downstairs on her way to school, both men gone to whatever job Edie's father had secured for them.

At high school Edie was significantly smarter than most of her classmates. She was going to graduate a year early, and then she was going to graduate in three years from Northwestern, which she would attend for free because her father worked there, and she would do magnificently, and then she would go to law school there, and there she would experience her first academic setback, and Edie would graduate merely in the middle of her class, maybe because her class consisted of an exceptionally bright group of people, maybe because the first year of law school her mother got sick, maybe because the second year of law school her father got sick, maybe because somewhere in the middle of that she met her someday-husband and fell in love, and maybe because there is only so much a woman can handle before she simply collapses.

But right then she was at the top of her game, her skin plum-tinted, her eyes glittering and dark, her hair soft and dark and curly and long enough to tie in a loose knot at her neck, tiny sprays of it fluttering out around her cheeks and jaw. She felt sharp and prestigious, and she had an understanding that she could do anything she wanted in the world, and that no one truly had the power at that moment in time to oppress her except for herself.

Big Edie Herzen.

"But there's something about a big girl, it's true. Even the really big ones," said Abraham.

"This is what I am trying to say," said Naumann. Edie didn't even know his first name.

Naumann, on the couch. Abraham in the basement. Her parents upstairs in bed.

Edie had only begun to engage in her flirtation with eating late at night. All day long it was this and that about Meir and Israel. Her father had smoked an entire pack of Pall Malls and had forgotten to eat. He was always so skinny. There were leftovers. There was half a loaf of rye bread, and there were so many delicious things to put between two slices of rye bread. Just sitting in the refrigerator, in the kitchen, past the living room.

She tiptoed downstairs, carpeting to tile to linoleum. The stench of cigarettes did not deter her from her goal. She would always think of cigarettes when she sat to eat. A lifetime of hating and loving a smell.

She did not even have to look around to know that it was Naumann who had lit up behind her and was now seated at the kitchen table. Edie had his number before he even opened his mouth. She could have touched him months ago. She could have run her finger along his swollen lips. Other girls did things like that all the time, and it was no big deal. Half her class had turned into hippies overnight. Her parents still loved each other, and held hands at the dinner table, and kissed each other good morning, good evening, and good night. There was nothing wrong with wanting another person, if it was the right person. But she had sized him up and given him a failing grade.

How could Naumann know this? He was too concerned with *her* size, what her ass would feel like if he squished each cheek between his hands, what her breasts would feel like if he put his face between them and pushed them up against his cheeks. What it would feel like to be with a girl he didn't have to pay for. He was also concerned with vodka. He was barely concerned with his job.

That spring, Edie's mother had hired someone to cut the bushes on the front lawn in unusual shapes, and through the side window Edie could see a dark green spiral in the moonlight. Coleslaw and roast beef between two slices of rye bread. She sat down at the table with Naumann and began to eat. He lit another cigarette. She felt fearless.

There was something about a big girl, after all.

"You are always so hungry," said Naumann, bitter but hopeful, lost in America, sleeping on a plastic-covered couch, waking up every night, without fail, on the living-room floor, grateful that at least the fall was carpeted. "You always have to have some food in your mouth."

Don't say it, thought Edie.

Edie's father had gotten Naumann a job cleaning the bathrooms at a high school in Winnetka. That meant he was a high-school janitor.

She took another bite. The coleslaw was creamy and tart.

Naumann inhaled deeply and drunkenly and then blew the smoke out his nose.

She could tell that he had no self-control. Neither did she in a lot of ways. She was sympathetic. But still. Don't say it.

"Maybe you need something else in your mouth," he said.

"Like I would screw someone who cleans toilets for a living," she said.

"You would be so lucky," he said. "Whore."

She finished her sandwich; she took her time, because she was hungry, and because it filled her up, and because she was in her house, in her kitchen, and she was a queen, and because women could rule the world with their iron fists. Then, when she was done with her sandwich, she let out a loud scream that surprised even her with its girlishness, and which woke her mother, and her father, and half the block, lights flinging on in bedrooms and living rooms, everyone stirred, everyone worried, everyone but Abraham, who slept through all the ruckus because he had taken his hearing aids out for the night. She felt not an ounce of regret. As far as she could tell, no great tragedy had occurred.

The Willow Tree

RACHELLE'S MOTHER-IN-LAW was not well. Rachelle wouldn't have described her as sickly, though, because there was nothing frail about her. Edie was six feet tall, and shaped like a massive egg under a rotating array of silky, shimmering housedresses that seemed to make her glow. But Edie had had stent surgery six months before on her rotting thigh—a side effect of diabetes—with another surgery scheduled in a few weeks, and also lately Rachelle had noticed that two of Edie's teeth had gone black. Concern stabbed her directly in the heart. Also, she was disgusted. Yet she could not bring herself to mention it.

It wasn't her job, anyway, to talk to her mother-in-law about dental care. She had a household to run, two children to take care of, a b'nai mitzvah to plan. (Everyone, everywhere, knew she had a b'nai mitzvah to plan, her hairstylist, her Pilates instructor, the kids' dance teacher, her girlfriends who had all waited to have children till their late twenties and were always one step behind her in the parenting department. "You think you have your hands full now," she would tell her old college roommates. "Just you wait.")

She was willing to support her mother-in-law in many ways. She happily sat by her side at the hospital for hours on end with her father-in-law, Richard, and her husband, Benny. When Richard was too busy at the pharmacy to tend to his own wife's needs, Rachelle would chauffeur Edie to check ups, to the Jewel and Costco for groceries. And she had cooked them meals in their home before heading home to feed her own family, sitting patiently through Edie and Richard's awful back-and-forth bickering about little nitpicky things, the fabric softener, lawn care, their finances, these arguments that always ended with Richard throwing up his hands and walking away and Edie turning to Rachelle and crooning gently, "Marriage is for the birds," and then making a chirping noise and smiling.

This, for her family, for her husband, she would do. She could do it, easily.

But nowhere was it in her job description as wife and mother and homemaker to be the one to let her mother-in-law know that her teeth were turning to shit.

"Why isn't your father saying anything?" she asked Benny. "Do you think he noticed?"

It was after dinner, and the kids were in bed, their last text messages sent for the night. Benny and Rachelle were out back. Benny was taking long puffs from the last remaining bit of a tiny pin joint. Rachelle was shivering like a small, precious, expensive dog. January in Chicago, they must be insane. The pool was covered with a tarp. They both wore large, insulated, puffy coats.

"You know as much as I do," said Benny.

It was the incisor on the bottom left, and the tooth next to it. They were both black at the root. Rachelle could see them only when Edie smiled, and she smiled a lot when the twins were around.

"Do we have to talk about this now?" he said. The chill of the air and the smoke from the joint united into one giant cloud. He ground out the rest of the joint under his shoe.

"When would you like to talk about it?" she said.

He put his hand at her neck lightly and then circled his hand around her hair into a ponytail. At any given moment, she could never be sure who was in control of their relationship.

"Never?" he said.

"She's your mother," she said. "You're not worried?"

"All I ever am is worried about her," he said sadly. His eyes widened, he made a tiny choking sound, and then he was crying. She threw her arms up and around him, and the two of them stood there in the cold embracing for a while, two puffy coats in the night. Between them hovered a shared thought: that they were in this together. And when one of them failed, the other must succeed.

"Maybe you could talk to her tomorrow?" he said finally. The prickle of his beard against her face as he spoke stimulated her.

"I could," she said. "I could do it while the kids are at dance class."

"There you go," he said softly.

For three weeks, the twins had been taking hip-hop dance lessons in preparation for their b'nai mitzvah, and they had made some progress, but Rachelle was worried they wouldn't be ready in time for the party, or worse, that they would embarrass themselves. The plan was for them to do a routine after dinner, followed by a video montage of the twins through the years. Then a dessert bar would be wheeled out, including a make-your-own sundae station and a bubbling chocolate fountain, surrounded by cookies, pound cake, and strawberries. Rachelle had seen those fountains before at other bar mitzvahs and once at a wedding, and she thought they were more trouble than they were worth—what a mess! Chocolate everywhere, but everybody had one at their parties now, and she would not disappoint her children, her babies, her miracles.

They had insisted on the dance lessons as well. They had no shot at singing, which some of their peers did for the performance portion of the party. Even Josh and Emily recognized that they would be setting themselves up for failure; Josh's voice was in the midst of some serious and dramatic changes, and Emily—brassy, deep-voiced Emily—had been rejected from the school chorus three years running. But they were diligent kids, and had both played soccer since grade school, and were fit and athletic, and they understood what it meant to show up and practice. They had promised to take it seriously. They had promised results.

And she trusted their instructor, Pierre, who had toured nationally and, in one instance, internationally, with a number of productions of Broadway musicals—this she had learned from scouring the Internet ruthlessly, because in a former life she had been a good student, a solid researcher, and also because she was not going to leave her kids for one hour a day, three times a week, with just any old person with tap shoes and a three-year lease on some office space.

She need not have worried, though, for Pierre was the real deal. He had moved to the area a few years earlier because his mother lived nearby and was sick with something terrible—Rachelle couldn't remember what, she wanted to say leukemia, who were all these people with all these awful diseases?—and then he had never left. "You've got to take care of your family," he had explained to her. "I mean, in the end that's all you've got, you know what I mean?" Rachelle had nodded furiously. He was speaking directly to her soul.

And though his dance studio was located in a dark corner of a sprawling business complex one block from the new Walmart on Route 83, once she entered it for the first time, she knew that this man was authentic and talented. It was just a simple space, with a small office in the front and a white-walled practice area. But the walls of the front room were covered with dozens of pictures of Pierre with celebrities, Broadway stars and pop idols and a handful of television actors. And these weren't staged photos either: There was Pierre on a beach, shirtless and smiling, his arms slender like firm, flat noodles, wrapped around another shirtless and smiling man; Pierre crammed in at a dinner table surrounded by fabulous people, his big, gentle eyes glittering; a sweaty Pierre post-performance with the rest of the cast, his smooth, cocoa-colored face caked with makeup, his smile exuberant. Rachelle could almost hear his heavy breathing through the picture, the rapid thump of his heart. He was the most exhilarating and thrilling person she had met in a long time.

But as she watched Josh and Emily at the end of each class through the window between the office and the practice space, she saw how awkward they still were. Josh seemed the better of the two; he could keep a rhythm, even if his motions were stiff. But Emily was off on every count, and sometimes she stopped and stared, silently mouthing the count, her eyes glassy, as Pierre repeated the same moves over and over. He never lost his cool, though; his voice was warm and encouraging, and when Josh had a minor triumph, he hooted, "Oooh, boy, you got it going on now."

Pierre promised her, "I'll turn them into solid gold," and she believed him. He knew Ricky Martin, after all.

The kids walked past their mother, their eyes glued to their iPhones—Hanukkah gifts from the previous month, against her better judgment, all those studies with the tumors and the cancer, she wouldn't even let them talk on them, only text—giving a quick good-bye to Pierre. "Don't forget to vote tonight," he said. "We won't," said Emily.

"You can vote, too," said Pierre. He pointed to a new picture on the wall, of him and a skinny young Asian man with pale blue eyes and a Mohawk. The two of them both had ice-cream cones, the tips of which were touching. Pierre explained the man was a former student of his who was now appearing on *So You Think You Can Dance*. He was in the finals, and he needed people to vote for him. "You can call or text," said Pierre. "If you're the texting type."

She wasn't, but she could learn to be.

The class lasted ninety minutes, and her in-laws' home—the same house where Benny had grown up with his sister, Robin—was ten minutes away from the studio. That meant Rachelle had at least an hour to spend with Edie, which seemed more than enough time to approach the matter of her teeth and perhaps even the larger looming issue of her health, which she had not attempted to change one bit even though her doctors, everyone around her, had issued serious warnings about it. Legs, teeth, heart, blood. Everything about her was collapsing. She weighed well over three hundred pounds. If she did not alter her diet and begin to exercise, she might die: the doctor had said as much to all of them. A bypass might soon be an inevitability rather than just a possibility. How many more surgeries would she have to have before she would change her life? Did she value her life so little? To Rachelle, to Benny, to everyone they knew, it was unimaginable. One surgery would have been enough for them.

Benny's father had said, uselessly, more than once, "You know your mother, I can't get her to do anything she doesn't want to do." And that was all he was willing to say on the matter. He simply was not willing to take on his wife. While Edie was wonderful to her own children, the grandchildren, and Rachelle herself, she pecked at Richard constantly, as if she were a sparrow and he was some crumb just out of reach; it made Rachelle like her less.

Still, Rachelle was certain it was Richard's responsibility to help his wife get healthy, and yet here she was, driving through one long subdivision of new homes, and then another, until she arrived at a tiny side street still full of homes that were built in the 1960s, the owners of which had never sold out to developers, or had sold directly to younger families. Every third house looked exactly alike. Many were ranch style, and they all had fenced-in backyards. In the warmer months, robust American elms bloomed in the front yards. It was a fine, quiet block. Rachelle had seen pictures of the house from thirty years ago, in family photo albums, Benny and Robin standing in front of a massive willow tree in soft petal bloom, Robin chubby, poky little breasts in a polo shirt, half smiling, squinting from the sun, and Benny with a Cubs hat and a baseball glove, a big grin, a brace face, sparkling next to his sister. How had Benny turned out so cheerful and Robin so sad? Nobody knew. It was in their genes; that's all anyone could guess. That willow tree was gone, and now there was just a low row of unevenly manicured bushes in front of the two-car garage, poorly maintained by Edie, who, in the spring, occasionally hacked at them with a giant set of clippers. "I do love the fresh air," she would say.

Rachelle parked across the street from the house, but did not get out of the car; her legs would simply not move, and she could not even bring herself to turn off the engine. *Unfair,* she thought, the word hotly blinking in her head, branding her with each throb. Why had she said yes? Because they were all in it together. Because her mission in life was to keep her family happy and healthy. Because where she failed, her husband would pick her up, and she would do the same for him. Just as she was doing now.

The front door to the house opened; it was Edie, wrapped in her enormous mink coat and matching hat, an inheritance from her own oversized mother. ("I am morally opposed to fur," Edie had told Rachelle once. "But since it's already here, what am I going to do? Throw it away?" Rachelle had fingered the coat delicately with her fine, manicured hand, and imagined having it taken in—dramatically—someday for herself. "You can't waste mink," agreed Rachelle.) Edie got into her car, and before Rachelle could get out of her own car to stop her, drove off.

Rachelle didn't hesitate. She followed her mother-in-law, past the high school—a digital marquee in front of the school flashing GO TEAM! again and again—until she pulled into a McDonald's parking lot. She made it through the drive-thru swiftly and then pulled out onto the road back to the subdivisions, but instead of heading home she went in the other direction, and Rachelle still followed her—she was morbidly curious at this point—this time into a Burger King, again through the drive-thru window, pausing before she exited back onto the main road in front of a garbage can in the parking lot, into which she tossed her now-empty, crumpled McDonald's bag through her window. A half beat later, she hurled an empty plastic cup. Perfect aim.

Edie continued driving farther from her house, and now Rachelle had transitioned into a pure sadness, her lips downturned gently, her mouth given in to the grief, a series of sighs floating delicately, resignedly through her nose. She turned off the heat in the car, and now the air was simply still. Edie turned in to a strip mall about a mile up the road and pulled up in front of a Chinese restaurant, dimly lit, barely open, and walked purposefully inside, stopping again briefly by a garbage can, where she deposited her Burger King bag. Rachelle watched as a young waitress greeted Edie with an excited hug.

She's going to die, thought Rachelle. *And I don't know if we can stop her.*

She thought about walking inside the Chinese restaurant, reaching up the half-foot distance between them, grabbing Edie by the collar of her beautiful coat, and demanding she stop—stop what? Stop eating? Stop eating *everything?* But to do that would be to admit that Rachelle had been following her for the last twenty minutes, and she would never do that.

Instead she turned her car back out onto the street and headed toward Pierre's studio, sub-division, subdivision, left, right, parked, and then watched the last twenty minutes of the twins' practice. They were so young and healthy and beautiful. They were thin. Emily looked a little like her Aunt Robin in the mouth, those sad, pursed, vaguely sexy lips. Josh was all Benny, dark, thick, bristly hair, surprisingly well-shaped eyebrows, a small but determined smile. She could see nothing in them physically that indicated that they would grow up someday and turn out like their grandmother, even if Emily did seem sullen sometimes, which was not necessarily a correlative to a negative relationship to food, but it was something that she, Rachelle, as a mother, could keep an eye on nonetheless.

While the kids packed up their gym bags at the end of class, she leaned on one side of the doorway, while Pierre leaned on the other. In her own quiet way, she began to beg for his approval.

"There's hope for them yet, right?" she said.

"They're just diamonds in the rough," he said, and he winked. "Waiting to emerge like beautiful little rainbows." He raised his hands to the sky and shimmered them down, and Rachelle followed the path of his fingertips down to his sides. She swore he had left little trails of pixie dust in the air behind them.

"And how about you, Miss Rachelle? How are you doing? That's a big party you've been planning."

She had bemoaned the chocolate fountain to him

in the past. The chocolate fountain felt excessive to Rachelle, and the thought of gallons upon gallons of chocolate hitting the air and then bubbling up in a pool made her nauseous. A gateway to cavities, at the least. But it wasn't about her, this party. It was about her kids, and about their family. "A little chocolate never hurt anyone," Pierre had told her, and he had laughed outrageously, and she had laughed too, even though she wasn't totally sure she had gotten the joke.

"The save-the-date cards go out next week," she said. "Well, they're actually little magnets." She pulled one out of her purse—JOSH AND EMILY B'NAI MITZVAH JUNE 5, 2010—TONIGHT'S GONNA BE A GOOD NIGHT!—and handed it to him. "You're invited, of course." She said this without thinking. Was he invited? She would love to see him on the dance floor.

"That's so sweet," he said evenly.

Rachelle blushed. "I'm sure you've got a busy schedule," she said. "And you probably get invited to lots of bar mitzvahs."

"Not too many," he said. "I think people are always worried about who I'm going to bring as a date." He laughed, his own private joke that wasn't so private.

"You can bring whomever you like," Rachelle said, and she meant it. She could not help but steal a glance at his gleaming wall of celebrity photos.

"I'll check my schedule," he said, and she felt deeply—she knew!—that he meant it, too.

Benny was already at home when she returned with the kids, setting the table, an Edwardo's box on the kitchen counter. He was still wearing his suit, an old one, the crease nearly faded in the pants. (She would donate it to the Goodwill tomorrow, she decided.) He must have just beaten them home. It was his one night to cook, and he had cheated and gotten a pizza.

"Tell me you at least got a salad," she said. "Something with nutritional value."

Benny pulled a large plastic container of salad out of a bag and waved it at Rachelle.

"What am I, crazy?" he said. "I don't want to spend the night in the doghouse."

"We don't have a doghouse," said Josh. "Or a dog."

"It's an expression," said Benny. "A joke. You're no fun. When did this kid turn into no fun?"

"He's plenty of fun," said Rachelle. "You should have seen him dancing tonight."

They all sat and ate, Benny barraging Emily and Josh with questions about their day, which sometimes they minded, and sometimes they didn't. He made a real effort with those kids, which Rachelle appreciated. Her own father, miserable, overworked, uninspired by his job, his wife, his child, his life, the world, had ignored her through most of her childhood; he would sit, stony-faced, at the dinner table, and command quiet through angry glares at Rachelle and her mother. "Your father had a bad day," her mother would whisper.

There would be no silence at the dinner table in her own home.

After dinner they all watched *So You Think You Can Dance*, and there was Pierre's student, Victor Long, spiked hair, bright eyes, jumping in the air, both legs flying up and out to meet his hands, tumbling, bouncing, knees popping up and down, all to a dance track that was punctuated occasionally by an intriguing air-horn sound. Victor was athletic and graceful, which Rachelle admired, even if she would never choose to dance that way herself. Her children were in awe of him.

"I'm never going to be that good," said Emily mournfully. She crossed her arms and locked her thumbs under her armpits. "I'm going to look like an idiot in front of all my friends."

"You're going to do the best that you can," said Rachelle.

"But what if my best totally sucks?" said Emily. She wiped away a tear, and another, and then got up and left the room, dragging Rachelle's heart slowly with her.

Later, out back, after the kids were tucked away in bed, Rachelle huddled in her winter coat with her husband in the backyard, both of them quietly puffing on a joint; this time she shared it with him. Benny needed it more than she. For him, it was something he earned at the end of a long day of work. For her, smoking pot was just for fun, usually, but following Edie that afternoon had saddened her, and she felt like she needed it, too, or even deserved it. Because what did she do all day anyway? She managed a household, and all their possessions. Drove her kids around, Pilates four times a week, an occasional Sisterhood meeting at the temple with all those old ladies who thought they knew everything about everything but only knew something about not much at all if you really wanted to get into it, got her hair done (regular bang trims, coloring once a month), her nails done, her toes, waxing, cooking, shopping. She read books. (She was in three book clubs but she only showed up if she liked the book they were reading.) If you asked her at the right time, she'd say, "Spend my husband's money." It was a joke. It was supposed to be funny. But it was true, too.

"So they're not getting any better?" he said.

"Josh isn't terrible," she said. "Emily's got no particular sense of rhythm as far as I can see."

"It's only been a few weeks," he said. He put his hand on her head. He messed up her hair.

"Don't," she said.

"Did you just get it done?" He rubbed it back

and forth and in her face. "Did you just get your pretty hair done?" He was completely high. He laughed. He ran his fingertips down her face and then stopped at her chin and squeezed it. "This is a good chin, here, this one." And then he kissed her.

She took the joint from his hand. "No more for you," she said. She put another hand in his pocket and felt for his dick. Managing his possessions.

He was in such a good mood that she didn't want to bring up his mother, but then he did it anyway.

"So did you see the other Mrs. Middlestein today?"

"Mrs. Middlestein Senior?"

"That's the one."

Here are the lies Rachelle had told her husband in the order she had told them:

1. When they first met, she had not yet broken up with Craig Rossman, her boyfriend who went to Cornell, and it was a good month before that happened, but she wanted to wait to do it in person, over Christmas break, and she could not be blamed for that, Craig was a decent guy, and doing it over the phone seemed callous.
2. When she was twenty-one and they first started dating, she said she was on the pill

when she was not because she didn't want him to think she was a total slut (this made no sense, she knew, everyone was on it, and at the least she could have said she did it to manage her cramps, but Benny thought she was an angel and she did not want him to think otherwise), and this led to her getting pregnant with the twins the night they graduated from college during a drunken, groping sexual rumble in a bathroom at a party at his frat house.

3. She is not a fan of her engagement ring, that teeny, tiny chip, and she faked it like a queen when he, hands shaking which was ridiculous, because he already knew that the answer was going to be yes, it had to be yes, offered it to her in a teeny, tiny red velvet box over dinner at a steak house in Chicago.

4. She lied when she said she thought his sister, Robin, was adorable the first time Rachelle met her. Robin was—and still is—miserable, moody, and weird, and Rachelle had never forgiven her for her inability to muster one decent smile for their wedding photos, not to mention the drinking—oh, the drinking! Was she the only one in the family who saw how much Robin drank?—and if she had her way she would cut Robin out of every single picture in the album.

5. She lies once or twice a month about going to matinees during the day by herself because she thinks he might begrudge her that pleasure when he works so hard himself, and this lie necessitates a double lie, one when he asks what she did that day, and two when they go to see a movie she has already seen and she has to pretend she hasn't seen it yet, which has led her husband to wonder if she has lost her sense of humor, or, in a more subtle way he has not been able to name yet, her capacity for joy, because she barely laughs at the jokes she already knows are coming.

6. And finally, she doesn't always love being a stay-at-home mom, but the other option, dealing with bosses and responsibilities and meetings in poorly lit rooms and office politics and all that other crap that Benny goes through (and she is grateful he does it) on a daily basis, sounds so appalling that she will gladly gush, "This is what I was born to do," to anyone who might ask, her friends, his parents, her Pilates instructor, the women at the Sisterhood meetings, even if she suspects there might have been another option, if only she had not let Benny just put it in for a second because it felt so good and never made him take it out again before it was too late.

And now this: No, she had not seen his mother. No one had been home.

"What's going on over there?" he said, his late-night high disappearing into the winter air.

"I don't know," she said. "They're your parents. You know them better than I do."

"Where was she?"

"Benny."

"What?" He ground something imaginary under his shoe.

There were many moments when she suggested things to her husband, mostly in such a way that it seemed like it was his idea to begin with, and there were moments when she called him on his bullshit, usually while teasing him, so as to take away the sting, and then there were moments— and these moments were rare, because he was a good man, and Edie and Richard had done an excellent job of raising him to be a man and to take the right course of action—when she told him what to do.

"You need to talk to your mother. Not me. You."

"I'll call my dad," he said.

"Do whatever," she said, and then she was done talking for the night.

The next morning, Rachelle and Benny watched as Emily and Josh stood out back near the pool, bundled up in winter coats, practicing their dance moves. A Black Eyed Peas song blared from a boom box perched on a deck chair. It was a lovely, crisp, winter day; the sun hung serenely in blue, windless skies. Emily counted off each beat out loud. Josh closed his eyes and concentrated. They were desperately trying to glide across the tiled patio.

Emily pulled off her winter cap, and Josh unraveled his scarf. Emily walked over to the boom box to restart the song, and in that quick moment Josh popped and locked in one beautiful, swift motion.

Rachelle drew in her breath.

"Did you see that?" said Benny.

"I did," she said.

"Takes after his old man," said Benny. He executed a wobbly moonwalk across the kitchen floor.

"Right," said Rachelle.

The boom box began blasting the same song again. Rachelle was starting to hate that song.

"So I was thinking I'd drive over to my folks' house today," he said. He barely looked at her. She had stiffed him in bed last night, curled up in the far corner, a pillow behind her to rebuff any approach.

Rachelle did not know if he wanted her approval or not. If she gave her approval, it was as if she had commanded and he had followed, which, obviously, was what had happened, but she didn't know if it was wise to wound him any further. If she didn't acknowledge him, he might think she was still mad at him, which she wasn't. In fact, she was more in love with him at that moment than in years. All of the recent stressors on their marriage, his slight disconnection from his mother's multiple surgeries, his inability to prepare or even merely purchase a significantly healthy meal for his children for months now, all of that was washed away with just one appropriate, adult decision.

She threw her arms around him and enmeshed her fingers in his hair and kissed him, hard, and for a while, long enough so that when their daughter looked up at them through the window, it inspired her to believe in love and the sanctity of marriage, if not for herself, at least for others.

Later, in the parking lot of Old Orchard—there was a sale at Nordstrom's, winter coats, 30 percent off—Rachelle began to plot how she would save her mother-in-law. It would require a commitment from her husband and obviously from Richard, more than anyone. They would all have to work together to get Edie back on track. Rachelle would happily prepare meals for her, healthy meals, and she knew a nutritionist who was affiliated with her Pilates studio. Or maybe she would just sign her up for Weight Watchers. Rachelle would drive her to the meetings herself, and sit with her if she felt it necessary. And Rachelle would give up her daytime matinees to go to the gym with Edie if it meant she would finally get some exercise. Hell, all she had to do was go for a walk every day! Even that little bit would help. But more than anything, it was really on Richard to make sure she wasn't sneaking trips to the fast-food joints. If that meant he had to work less, then so be it. There was always time to make more money, but you only have one wife, and one life. And Benny would have to call his mother every single day and check in on her, and let her know that he loved her. A call from a son means everything to a mother. Rachelle knew she would want the same thing someday.

They were all in this together, that was the most important thing. If everyone worked together, Edie had a shot.

At the dance studio, the kids were sweating and grinning; Emily, in particular, had a healthy glow to her.

"Mom, we had a breakthrough moment," she said.

"They did," said Pierre, and he put his arm around Emily. "They remembered all their steps without me having to remind them."

"I could feel the whole thing inside me," said Josh. He touched his fingertips to his temples and then pressed hard, his eyes bugging out a bit. "Like I can see it all in my head."

"It's magic when it clicks like that," said Pierre.

Rachelle drank in all their energy, she felt it ripple through her face and neck and chest, a warm, milky love, and it melted into the enthusiasm she already had for turning her mother-in-law's life around. The kids were jumping up and down. Everyone was laughing. Rachelle pulled out her checkbook to pay Pierre for the month of classes. She asked him for a pen. He opened a desk drawer, and she saw inside at least a hundred different save-the-date magnets, all with different names on them. A pile of invitations. Of course everyone invited him. He was the most fabulous person ever. Rachelle blushed, and then felt a little nauseous. She wrote the amount incorrectly on the first check, and then tore it up, her hands trembling. *This is so dumb,* she thought. *What do I care? I have a mother-in-law to save.*

Benny returned just before dinner, sad creases worming their way around his forehead. He saw the kids and he smiled, and he hugged Emily, though over her head he gave a wary glance to Rachelle. Something began to tick inside her.

They ate salmon, bright pink, flavorless, and Rachelle eyed everyone as they reached for a pinch of salt, anything to save this meal, and she whispered, "Not too much." Brown rice. "Drink more water," she commanded. Out-of-season strawberries and sugarless cookies that sucked the air out of their lives. There would be no fooling around with food on her watch.

They bundled together in the living room, for the last night of *So You Think You Can Dance*, Rachelle on the sectional next to Emily. Rachelle stroked the top of her daughter's head. Emily had showered before dinner, and smelled good; Rachelle could tell she had used her shampoo. Her son was on the floor below them, his knees hunched up to his chest, rapt excitement at the upcoming revelation. Her husband was on the settee, stretched out like a dead man, his hands clasped across his belly. Rachelle looked at his gut. Was he getting a gut? Was everyone going to have to go on a diet around here?

During the final commercial break, Rachelle asked her husband, at last, how he was doing, and from across the room he let out a long, whiny, "Ehhh."

In the last moments of the show, the host announced Victor as the winner. The kids jumped up and down and screamed, and even Rachelle found herself clapping, while Benny did nothing but move his hands from his chest to behind his head. Confetti fell all around Victor as he hugged the host tightly. He swiped his thumbs under his eyes. He took the mike from the host and said, "I just want to thank everyone for making this happen. The viewers for all their support and for voting for me, my parents for believing in me, Jesus Christ our Lord and Savior, and my first dance instructor, Pierre Gonzales, for making me into the man I am today." And with that he gave a giant wink at the camera. A giant dirty wink? A giant wink. Rachelle didn't know. "Huh," she said. She looked over at her husband, who, for the first time that night, had cracked a smile.

Out back, under the stars, spring was so far away, months to go. Even longer till the kids had to get up in front of a roomful of people and pretend they were Victor Long for the night.

"What happened today?" she asked her husband. The joint was thicker than usual, and he had been outside long before she got there. He sat on a deck chair, his head on one hand, twirling the joint in the other.

"My father left my mother," he said.

"What are you talking about?" she said. That didn't even make any sense.

"He gave up on her," he said. "He said he couldn't take it anymore. He said he couldn't watch her kill herself anymore. He said she's a miserable woman and he couldn't live with her another day. She's having a meltdown."

He looked at his wife for help. He couldn't do this alone, and maybe he wouldn't even be able to do it with her help.

"He can't just leave," she said. Who just leaves a sick person? Nobody.

"He left," he said. "He seems pretty set on it. He rented an apartment near the pharmacy."

Rachelle walked over to her husband and sat in his lap, she wrapped one arm around his chest, and another, loosely, around his neck. Then she told him that she didn't want his father anywhere near her children. "Do you hear me?" she said. She said that any man who would abandon a sick woman was a filthy, horrible person and should not be allowed near a child. And he should be punished. And that is his punishment. He would have no access. He had gone insane, and he would have no access. Not her children. Not this man. Her husband argued briefly—who was in charge here anyway? was it him? did he even want to be?—but it was swift, and then it was over, because she raised her voice, she raised it loud enough that Josh heard it through his window. Josh, who had been thinking about Victor Long intently at that moment, wondering what would happen if he decided someday that he didn't want to be a doctor and wanted to be a dancer instead, if his parents would believe in him the same way, heard his mother screaming at his father, "I will not have him in my home! I will not have him in my life!" over and over until his father had no choice but to give her what she wanted.

Edie, 160 Pounds

THEY WERE SUPPOSED to meet for a burger at a folk-music club called the Earl of Old Town at 7:00 P.M., but then her father's test results were scheduled to come in sometime that evening, maybe the next day—the unpredictability of the timing, of everything, driving Edie into knotted bursts of tears in the bathroom attached to her father's hospital room—so she called her blind date and asked, nicely, if they could dine earlier in the evening and also somewhere near the hospital instead.

"What a shame," he said. "I heard that place was the place to go."

"For what?" she said.

"I don't know," he said. "For fun."

"What does it matter where we eat?" she snapped.

"I just wanted to try something new," he said.

"Look, I don't even know you," she said. "I don't know what's new or old for you."

"This is us, getting to know each other," he said, and then he started laughing at her, and she was appalled, because nothing was funny in this world, in her life, nothing.

Her mother had died the winter before, coldly, a

stroke, a coma, and one day of lucidity where she faintly clung to her family members, smiling, speechless, and then she was gone. The view from the hospital room was of a parking lot, and it had snowed the night her mother had her stroke. Edie had watched an old man shovel snow the next morning, making small mountains around the edges of the lot. By the time her mother died, the snow piles were covered in filth.

Now her father was entrenched in a bed at Northwestern Memorial; strings had been pulled to get him closer to his daughter, who attended the law school a few blocks away, one Russian calling another, a private room arranged for a good man. So in addition to her everyday back-and-forth between law school and library, there was also travel between her dorm and the hospital, up the elevators, down the hallways, through the doors. Edie just spent all day (when she was not sitting in class or studying in the library) walking, sometimes running. She could barely remember to eat, let alone that she should try and find a husband at some point, something her next-door neighbor, Carly, thought was extremely important. (Weren't they supposed to be feminists? Edie did not even have the energy to argue with her.)

She wasn't living any kind of life at all, but she was still more alive than her father, whose skin in the last few weeks had simply turned gray, his nose and ears becoming more pronounced against his shrinking head, even though none of his doctors knew exactly what was wrong with him. And this guy, her date, so leisurely, so cavalier, he had all the time in the world to try out new restaurants, didn't he?

"Can you just meet me at my dorm at six and let's not argue about it?" she said. "I'll be in front of the building."

"How will I recognize you?" he said.

"I'll be the one who doesn't care where we eat dinner," she said.

She did care. She missed eating. (Men, she didn't miss. You can't miss something you never had in the first place.) Food had been something that had made her happy, and now she was so sad and tired all the time that she could not even remember the connection between the two, between food and joy, and when she looked in the mirror, she saw drawn skin on her face, and unfamiliar bones across the top of her chest, delicately poking against her skin like shells beneath sand. Now food was merely something she used to power her body so that she could walk: dorm, class, dorm, hospital, dorm. Thirty years later she will lose track of distinct emotions, everything will be blurred together, and there will only just be feeling and eating. But for now food, along with joy, had slipped away from her.

And here was a man she didn't know—a fix-up; Carly had met him at shul, this Richard

Middlestein, and he had boldly asked her out, not noticing the glittering engagement ring on her finger, and when she had waved it at him, he had ducked his head, covered with thick, curly hair, awkwardly but charmingly, and he was tall and wearing a suit (no hippie, this one, thank God; hippies were over), and he was going to be a pharmacist in a year, and did he want to meet another smart Jewish girl? Of course he did!— taking the time to ask her what she wanted to eat. Maybe, Edie, you could slow down for a minute and answer the man?

"We could go to Gino's," she said.

"I love Gino's," he said. "I think Chicago pizza is better than New York pizza, and I say that as a lifelong New Yorker. But don't tell anyone I said that."

"Who would I tell?" she said.

Three hours later she leaned against the limestone walls of Abbott Hall, in a cool green summer dress that hung around her waist. A year ago it had fit her snugly across her gut and around her hips. She had been six feet tall for a few years, and had had a lovely plush body, and now she felt like a scarecrow. Where had her breasts gone? Those were mostly missing. Where were her parts? They had been disappeared by some unknown force. She turned her head right and noticed the lake, a handful of pristine sailboats gliding in the wind. Usually she never looked past the traffic speeding by on Lake Shore Drive. Carly had gone sailing with her rich, cerebral fiancé two weeks ago and had invited her along, and Edie had declined the offer before Carly had even finished her sentence. She was going to be an orphan soon: her father was dying, she was sure of it. His first test had been inconclusive, but deep in her heart she knew that all those Pall Malls had taken their toll, and it was not nickels or dimes her father would pay. Do orphans even go sailing?

Other law students exited the building, books in hand. They were all going to do better than her in class, in life. She had so much work to do, and she couldn't catch up; she was, for the first time ever, only a merely adequate student. She didn't even know what kind of lawyer she wanted to become. She should know by now what she was going to be someday. Why was she going to eat pizza with a stranger?

She wore her hair down, a good idea, the dark curls a tantalizing contrast with her green dress, and she had dug out a small bottle of lip gloss from the bottom of her underwear drawer, where it had fallen six months before and where she had not so accidentally forgotten about it, as if even the slightest lick of makeup would slow her down.

And then there he was, in a suit (it was his only suit, but she didn't know that yet), and he was smiling (his happiest days were behind him the minute he met her, but he didn't know that yet), and tall, much taller than Edie, so that she felt even smaller, and he walked confidently, like he liked what he had swinging between his legs. And the curly hair she had been told about was indeed thick and dark, just like her own hair, and so he instantly felt familiar to her. A different kind of woman might not have wanted the familiar. Five years down the line, who knows? Maybe Edie would have become that kind of woman, who wanted nothing to do with someone who came from the same place. He might have been from New York City, but he was just the same as she was. As her father hovered on the edge of something terrible, as he dwindled down into a pale, bony version of his former self, as he threatened to disappear entirely, here was a man who was tall and healthy and full of something Edie found herself wanting to devour.

"Let's go," she said.

But how far did they make it? One block, two blocks, and then they were approaching the hospital. And then how many steps past the hospital until she felt her gut pull her back toward her father? Even though he had encouraged her to go meet this young, single, Jewish man. "The test results will be the same no matter what time of day," he told her. But she stiffened like stone on the corner of St. Clair Street, the wind pushing back at her dress and her hair, frozen and alive at the same time.

Here was what she wanted to say to this Richard, making his jokes, touching her elbow: *Did you know that my father translated three books of Russian poetry into English? For fun, he did it. It wasn't even his job. He just loved poetry. I have the books. I can show them to you. The titles are embossed in gold.*

Here is what she would have said to this Richard, looking at her lips: *All he ever did was love my mother and help people.*

Here is what she would have said if she felt like herself, whatever that meant anymore: *A life well spent, do you know anything about that?*

Instead she said, "My father is sick." Still looking at him, she pointed her hand faintly in the direction of the hospital.

And he said, "I heard."

"I can't eat," she said.

"You gotta eat," he said kindly, and now both of his hands were on her arms. "I'm going to take care of this," he said.

And that was how Edie and Richard's first date ended in a hospital room, a mushroom pizza from Gino's on the nightstand, Edie's father coughing and laughing at every single one of Richard's jokes, everyone in the room pretending that Edie did not twice excuse herself to the bathroom to cry. It was the story Edie told at their ten-year-anniversary party, when there was still a chance they were in love. "He did not abandon me in my time of need," she said to their friends gathered before them in a private room at a suburban steak house. "It was the beginning of everything." Everyone raised a glass. To love, they said. To love.

Middlestein in Exile

"On THE ONE hand," said Richard Middlestein, Jew, local business owner, ex–New Yorker, "my wife and I were married for close to forty years, and we had built a life together, a home, a place in our community with our friends and family, a role in the synagogue." He had to admit that his relationship with the synagogue had diminished in the last few years for a variety of reasons, not the least of which was his wife's health. "And there were the kids to consider, although I didn't think Robin would care that much, and I thought, hey, Benny has his hands full keeping that wife of his happy. Isn't he busy enough? Maybe it would impact the grandkids, but how much?

"On the other hand," said Richard Middlestein, newly single gentleman, not-quite senior citizen, respectable, dull but fighting it, "my wife, who is a very smart woman who has done a lot of good for a lot of people so I can't totally knock her, my wife made me miserable, she picked at me till I bled on a daily basis, so much worse lately, more than you could ever imagine. And she got fat, so fat I could not love her in the same way anymore. Don't get me wrong, I like a little meat on the bones. I knew what I was marrying. But she was hurting herself. Every day, more and more. That is hard on a person. To watch that happen." He lowered his voice. "And it had been a long time since we'd had marital relations."

He could not bring himself to explain further that he had imagined that his sex drive would fade away in his late fifties and he would just forget that they had been sleeping on opposite sides of the bed, clinging to their respective corners as if they were holding on to the edge of a cliff. But sixty came, and his sex drive still simmered insistently within him, unused but not expired, a fire in the hole. He had never cared before, but now suddenly he realized that he could not go the rest of his life without sex, that he refused to give up the fight. But he knew also he would never want to touch his wife's pocked, veined, bloated flesh ever again. If not now, then when?

"I felt I had no choice but to leave her. The divorce is going to be final in six months, more or less." (More.) "I'm sure you understand."

The woman he had met on the Internet, a good-looking redhead named Jill, a legal secretary in her early fifties who had lost her husband, the love of her life, three years earlier—drunk-driving accident (not him, the other guy)—who was having a hard enough time with dating and would give anything to have her husband back even for a day, no, she did not understand. She clasped her hands together and looked down and thought about her wedding day in 1992, a small ceremony in Madison, where she was born and raised, and she pictured, as she had been doing far too much lately—it was not *healthy,* she could admit it—her husband bent down at her leg, sliding off her garter while everyone she loved in the world laughed and applauded.

As with every previous failed Internet date, Middlestein picked up the check.

Middlestein had been meeting women online for three months, since the day he had left his wife, leaving practically everything behind, books, furniture, photo albums, any record of the past. He had moved into the new condo building across the street from the pharmacy he owned, an apartment which he had signed a lease on two months before he left her and had been quietly furnishing by making secret trips to the IKEA in Schaumburg. Three times he had steered his cart through the crush of traffic in the dizzyingly bright aisles, at first awkwardly, this new singular decision-making identity unfamiliar. (His wife had made all household decisions since the day they'd married, crushing him like a nut when he offered the slightest opinion—and had he really cared? No, probably not, but he would never know now.) But with each successive trip, he had a renewed confidence: The Swedish names were meant not to confuse but to guide; he was not required to make a buying decision until nearly just before he reached the cash register, and even then he had the power to walk out the door without a single item in his cart; and maybe he did want a color scheme after all. Maybe he was a color-scheme kind of guy.

And what a bargain that place was! Sure, it was a lot of crap he didn't need, and his father, who had owned a high-end furniture shop in Jackson Heights for decades, would probably roll over, coughing, grumbling, cursing, in his grave if he saw what Richard's new bed frame was made of. But he was not a rich man—by some standards, maybe, to starving children in India, he probably lived like a king—since the market had wiped out half their retirement fund, so he had no choice in the matter.

Now he had a slickly furnished condo (white and dark blue with this little crisscross patchy pattern on all his bedding and pillows) and his heart and his life up on a screen for anyone to see. He exploited his newfound freedom at first, dating daily, sometimes twice a day, meeting one woman for lunch and another for dinner. There were thousands of women between the ages of forty and fifty-five (he didn't want to date a woman his own age, he wanted them young and vital and alive and ready to keep up with him—with how he was imagining he was going to be—once they finally hit the sack together) who were Jewish, divorced, widowed, never married, living within forty miles of his zip code (anything farther and he'd be dating a Wisconsin girl, and that didn't feel right to him; he didn't even *know* if there were Jews in Wisconsin anyway), though he was, if he had to be honest, more attracted to people within a twenty-mile range, because traffic was such a mess these days with so much construction going on. And all he had to do, apparently, was ask, and they would be willing to meet him. There were a lot of lonely ladies out there looking for love. *Good,* he thought, *more for me.*

He had dated fifteen divorcées, some more bitter than others, even more bitter than his wife, but they were also the funniest out of all the women he met, their pain somehow strengthening them, the endless paperwork and court proceedings and therapy sessions forcing them to look inward and, if not good-naturedly then at least wryly, laugh at themselves and the situation they were in. These women were veteran first-daters. They were putting themselves out there. They were hustling to meet their new mate.

He dated a dozen widows, most of whom had sopped up their tragedies like their hearts were sponges. They did not want to be on that date. They were there because someone had made them, their child, their mother, their sister, their co-worker. If they had their way they would stay home by themselves on a Friday night, but could

81

they really stay home on every Friday night for the rest of their lives? In their ads they promised they were lively and active and engaged in the world around them, but in person they were only able to fake it for a half hour or so before their devastation became apparent to Middlestein. On three occasions his dates had cried. They had his sympathy. He acted the part anyway. But eventually he began to grumble to himself, *If you're not ready to date, then why are you here?* He didn't want to be anyone's practice run. He hadn't dated a widow in a month, crossed them off his list of potential mates, but that redhead looked so gorgeous in her photo, ooh, she had that gorgeous bosom and gigantic eyelashes, he could just see himself getting caught up in her, if only she hadn't wanted to leave in such a hurry.

The rest were these women who had never married. At first he thought of them as these *poor* women, because how their egos must have suffered as they careened through their free-flying youth and suddenly woke up one day to realize they had become old, Jewish maids. Also, they had never experienced what it was like to be committed thoroughly, which, for better or worse, had taught him a thing or two about life and shaped the man he had become. But sometimes after talking for a while, he thought maybe they were the lucky ones. They weren't ruined like the rest of the women, at least not in the same way.

Their losses were different, and what they had gained was different, too. Most of them were childless. Most of them could give or take marriage, and he suspected that when they left him, they never gave him another thought. His picture was blurry, but there was no denying it in person. Even if he had molded his interests in his profile to match the ads of the younger women, one look and they knew, this guy had never done yoga in his life, and most likely was not picnicking in Millennium Park either. He was somebody's father, somebody's grandfather; an old man.

And then there was the hooker, or half a hooker, maybe; he wasn't quite sure what she was. Tracy had contacted him on the site a few days after he joined it, and he should have suspected something, because she was far younger than him, thirty-nine years old—only four years older than his son! What would she want with him anyway? He should have known, but still he agreed to meet with her, suggesting coffee, then she suggesting a drink, and then a few hours before they were to meet, she e-mailing him and telling him she had just come from the gym and had had a tough workout and she was *famished* and did he mind meeting her for dinner instead? She named a pricey steak house, and how could he say no? He didn't want to seem cheap or less than a class act.

She turned out to be a real knockout—though

perhaps a bit older than she claimed on her profile—with dark, shining eyes, plump lips, a lush behind, and slick, minklike hair that she kept pulled to one side over her bare shoulder. She was wearing a strapless dress made of a black stretchy material that ended above the knee. Middlestein hadn't seen that much skin on a woman up close in a long time. She smelled fantastic, this combination of flowers and baby powder, and she was tan, and fit, and everything about her was perfect. As she slowly crossed and uncrossed her legs and ran her fingertips along the shiny enameled wood of the bar, possibilities unfolded in front of him.

They sat first at the bar—she guzzled a martini, he sipped at a beer—until their names were called, and he couldn't say exactly what was going on until after they had been seated and just before their steaks had already been delivered. He asked if she enjoyed her work as a receptionist at a massage-therapy institute, and she put her hand on his and said, "Well, what I'm really looking for is a daddy, so I never have to work again," and then she giggled, and he stared at her for longer than he meant to, and she said, "If you know what I mean," in a low voice, and he—he just couldn't help himself—he did the briefest of calculations, he moved a zero around in his bank account, even though he already knew the answer, and this was not what he wanted anyway, but oh, he wouldn't mind putting his hands on that *tuchus* of hers. But there was no way. A steak dinner, sure; not much more than that, though. And if he couldn't bring her to his grandchildren's b'nai mitzvah in June— he could just hear the whispers, he knew he'd be whispering himself if one of his buddies did the same, and his children, and especially that daughter-in-law of his, would never forgive him—then she wasn't much of an investment at all. Then she said, "Do you think you would like to be my daddy?" and a massive pang of depression struck him, and he looked down into the bottom of his drink, searching deeply for his dignity. When he looked up, her smile had faded.

"I'm just looking to meet a nice lady," he said, which wasn't exactly true, but was closer to the truth than what she was proposing.

"I can be very nice," she said, the last remnants of her flirtation fading, because she was not there to defend herself, only to promote her possibilities.

And then there were the steaks, and they were delicious. She took half of hers home in a doggy bag, which she clutched to herself as they stood in the parking lot. A kiss on the cheek, and then a whisper: "You know how to reach me if you change your mind."

He had her number in his hand right now and was thinking about giving her a call after the day, week, month, year, life he'd had. A few hours after his depressing coffee date with Jill—who had left in tears, though thankfully she'd waited until she got in her car for the real waterworks to start; he had seen her sobbing at the stoplight—he met his daughter, Robin, for dinner. He hadn't seen her since he'd left his wife, only spoken with her on the phone. The kids had circled their mother and had shut him down, Benny much more than Robin, but that was to be expected. Benny's wife, that obsessive, tightly wound, Little Miss Prim and Proper, was *outraged* that he had filed for divorce, as if no one had gotten divorced before, as if she knew everything there was to know about family and marriage and life, as if she were the moral arbiter of what was right and wrong when she was the one who had gotten knocked up even before she had graduated from college and she should consider herself lucky that she'd had a free ride practically since the day she had met his son. He could go on. He did not appreciate being judged.

"She doesn't want you in our lives," said Benny stiffly on the phone. "You're my father, and I have made it clear that I will continue to have a relationship with you. I think things just need to cool off. She'll calm down." It was shocking to Middlestein that he would no longer be able to see his beloved grandchildren regularly. He hadn't considered that such a thing would even be a possibility. He thought they would understand how he couldn't live with that woman any longer. Surely they knew what he went through. Surely they could accept that he had been in pain. But they had not; they treated him as if he were a criminal, like he had murdered someone, when his wife, Edie, was the one killing herself, and taking him with her piece by piece.

His daughter was only slightly more reasonable, but first she had to get her anger out of the way. She had been like that since the day she was born: a screamer, a howler, and then she would slide, herky-jerky, into something resembling acceptance. He didn't get her, he knew that much. He didn't know why he needed to get her anyway. His father had never gotten him. Why did people need to be *gotten* so much? Why couldn't they just accept that he had left his wife and respect his decision? Why did he need to justify his existence to anyone?

It seemed like that was all he was doing lately. What he wanted to say to his daughter was, *I don't have to explain myself to you.* Up until now, he had been able to say that to her his entire life, and whether she agreed or not, he was going to take that action. Now the dynamic had changed. He needed her—what did he need her for, exactly? He needed her so that he could stay connected to his family. He needed her to speak well of him to Benny, so that he could see his grandchildren again. And, even though he shouldn't have to explain himself to anyone, even though he was the father and she was the child and she should just listen to him, he needed to know she didn't hate him so that he could sleep at night. Because lately he had been taking an Ambien or two before bedtime, and even sometimes mixing it with scotch, and who knew what would be next? For a while he blamed his insomnia on his new bedding. The sheets weren't soft, the mattress too stiff. He was running out of things to blame it on, and he could not, he would not, blame it on himself.

They met for dinner, at a middling Thai restaurant near the train station, where his daughter, a thin girl (maybe too thin for her own good after a tubby childhood), a moody girl, a smart girl, began to rattle off his failures.

"She is *dying,* literally killing herself, and you have just abandoned her as if your life together, and her life in general, is of no consequence."

She had her mother's eyes, he noticed for the millionth time, black little balls of fury. Seeing the familiar, seeing her eyes, it had touched him; it had been sixty-plus days since he had seen anyone he was related to.

"What about my life?" he said. He resisted pounding his fist on the table, though he felt as if some sort of extra punctuation was required to make his point, and a nice, solid physical gesture sometimes seemed right. Once he had punched a hole in the wall of the garage after an argument with Edie. But that was years ago, when he still fought with her, when she could still incite him to give a shit about winning. "Doesn't my life have value? Don't I deserve to be happy?"

"Of course you deserve to be happy," she said; and he thought maybe she might be softening, but it was hard to tell with her. "We all deserve to be happy." Was that almost a smile? But then it was gone. "This is life, though, and—I can't even believe I have to say this to you, because you are the father and I am the child and I feel like you should know how this works." She seemed nauseated. She practically gagged, then restrained herself. "You deserve to be happy, yes. But life is not always easy! And when the going gets tough and the chips are down—I know you do not need to hear all these clichés to get the point—you need to stand up for the people in your life, and that especially includes the woman you've been married to for forty years. She's your wife, Dad! Your wife!"

He had never had dinner with his daughter before, he suddenly realized. Not one-on-one. She had her tête-à-têtes with her mother every few months or so. But it would never have occurred to him before this moment to pick up the phone and call her and ask her out to dinner. (Did he even call her? He wasn't sure. It seemed like it had been a lifetime of his wife making the calls and then handing the phone to him at the tail end of the conversation, he making a few gruff comments about his job, she pretending to care, the two of them forgetting about their exchange the instant it was over. His wife would let him know when there was something he should be worried about.) He supposed this was it, for the rest of his life. Dinner in a series of dingy but serviceable ethnic restaurants, beneath a giant framed print of a waterfall cascading into a beach, the bottom of the photo stained slightly by some sort of red sauce.

"Here's the question, Dad, and this is the biggie," she said. She ran her fingers up her sinewy arms, stroking a thin but solid blue vein protruding from beneath the skin. This seemed like an unattractive habit at best to Middlestein, and the kind of thing that might scare a man away. But it was none of his business if she got married or not. Maybe once upon a time, but he knew he would never be able to say a thing to her again about it. She looked up, looked him in the eye, and said, "Do you think she would ever do the same to you? Leave you when you needed her most?"

"Robin, your mother left me a long time ago," he said, and whether Robin knew it, or Benny knew it, or that ballbuster of a wife of his knew it, it was true.

"When?" she said.

"It has been a lifetime of whens," he said.

And then he refused to discuss it any further,

dissect his marriage for his daughter, because it was enough already, and the food had arrived, and could they just eat and stop fighting for a second? But he did get her to agree to see him again sometime, and to maybe put in a good (but not great) word for him with her brother, and he thought he had successfully convinced her to hate him slightly less than she did when the meal had started, until just before they said good-bye to each other in the parking lot, when he said, "So how is she? Your mother," and she looked like she was going to kill him, take those powerful arms of hers, her veiny hands, and wring his neck. "How do you think she is?" was her only response, and then she walked off—no hug, no kiss, nothing— toward the train station in the early spring chill, lean, hateful, angry, young, alive.

He had Tracy's number in his phone, but it was almost nine, and he decided it was too late to call. It wouldn't hurt to send an e-mail, though. Either she was up and would get it, or she'd get it tomorrow, and maybe by then he might have a change of heart. *I wouldn't mind seeing you again.* She replied almost immediately—"I'm game if you are," followed by a winking, blushing smiley face (even her choice of emoticon was seductive, thought Middlestein)—and, to his surprise, invited him over immediately. He hadn't expected such a quick response to his e-mail. Even some of the women he had met who didn't work (there were more than a few living on spousal support or inheritance) held on to some semblance of propriety and made him wait a few days to meet even though there they were, online, just like himself, obviously not doing a damn thing with their time. He suspected he knew what it all meant, but he also wanted to make no assumptions, because he didn't want to get into any tricky kind of trouble. He was no fool. He watched *Law & Order*, he watched *Dateline*. He knew about blackmail and con games and the like. But this was the furthest he had gotten with any woman yet, and they were in the suburbs of Chicago not Manhattan, and he was obviously not a rich man, maybe even she could see that he was not a bad man, even though he had left his sick wife all alone (which in the quietest moments in the mornings, alone in bed, he knew was a truly terrible thing), and was there any possibility that maybe she liked him a little bit? Was that the craziest thing in the world?

These are the things Middlestein told himself as he drove to the half hooker's house, the things that might make what he was doing okay in his book. If a friend of his told him he had done the same, Middlestein would like to think he wouldn't have judged. World's oldest profession. Biblical. Don't knock it till you try it.

She lived two towns over from him; the streets

were empty, and he arrived at her condo fifteen minutes early—now *there's no traffic,* he thought, *just when I could use a little traffic*—so he drove around in circles for a while; past a massive Kmart with a gardening center that made him sentimental for his backyard, even though his wife would never let him touch a thing; strip mall, strip mall, strip mall; a drive-through hot dog stand, which he contemplated visiting, only he didn't want hot dog breath; the high school his grandkids would attend in two years, and where he hoped he would see them graduate—they were both so bright, he bragged about them to everyone he knew, they were the best thing that had happened to their family in a long time and he was going to fight till the end to make sure he got to have them in his life, his daughter-in-law be damned—and then, after exactly seven minutes, he turned around and headed back to Tracy's condo, past the sparkling, bubbling fountain in front, parking in a guest spot as instructed, and finally hustling his way up to her apartment. He was more eager than he had realized, and he found himself out of breath before he reached the last flight of stairs. *Is this really happening?* he asked himself. *Yes, it is.*

She greeted him with a kiss on the cheek and a gentle hand on his arm. She was wearing this sort of half-slip kind of top. It looked like lingerie but also it could just be a really nice shirt—what did he know about fashion? It was pink, and she had blown her black hair straight, so it was even longer than usual. The black fell against the pink silkiness, and it looked phenomenal. His penis grew slightly hard.

Inside, a plinky jazz song played. Her apartment was three times the size of his. *Can I even afford her?* It was done up in a frilly decor, with a hodgepodge of antiques that looked as if she had gone from house to house over a series of decades and plucked just one piece of furniture from each: There was a long, narrow, modern glass kitchen table with plastic white chairs, and a molded plywood chair next to a shag rug, a diner-style table in the coffee nook, a club chair, a Mission oak armoire, piece after piece jammed next to one another, and that was just in the first room he entered. In the middle of it all was a giant red velvet fainting couch, and it was there that Tracy directed him to sit. She probably lay on it all the time, he thought, and he pictured her lying on it dramatically, little puffs of breath emanating slowly from her mouth.

"This is a nice place," he said.

"Thanks," she said. "I inherited it."

On a tiny bronze coffee table next to the couch, there was a framed picture of her with a white dog. Middlestein pointed to it. "Adorable," he said.

"She was," said Tracy. "Mitzi died a year ago." She jutted out her lower lip and made a sad face. "It was sad," she said. "I'm saving up to buy a new one, but they're so expensive. She was a bichon frisé. I always have bichons frisés. I've had three. You have to go through a breeder, you know. You should never use a pet store."

"Oh, yeah, why not?" he said.

"They're so mean to the puppies," she said, and she looked sincerely distressed. She snapped out of it almost instantly. "Let's not talk about this. It's depressing. Let's talk about happy things. Like you and me." She put one hand on his knee and the other in his hand. "I knew you wouldn't be able to stay away. I had a feeling about you." She kissed him.

This was an out-of-sight kiss for Middlestein for two reasons: one, because he was not expecting it, and second, because that Tracy was a phenomenal kisser. She had soft but firm lips, and she was good at reading men and knew instinctively what they wanted, whether they wanted to be in charge or whether she needed to take control. She made gentle noises of joy, or dark dirty laughs, whatever she thought they needed to hear. This translated into the bedroom of course, too. She'd be on top, bottom, sideways, whatever. She hadn't enjoyed sex in years, what did she care anyway? Much older men had ground that desire out of her since she'd been a teenager. She just wanted a new dog. Why hadn't anyone bought her a dog yet? Maybe this guy would buy her a dog, what was his name again?

Middlestein let himself be consumed by the kiss for a moment longer, and then his mind wandered to his current self, his physical form, his sixty-year-old body, which was still lean enough—he had been a runner for years, at least until his knees gave out a few years ago—but sagged in parts. He had an old-man chest, the flesh around the nipples puffy yet drooping, and he had gray hair everywhere, on his chest and back and around his penis. He wasn't terrible-looking naked, but there was no hiding who he was either. He didn't know if he could contend with even a glimmer of disappointment on Tracy's practiced expression. Then he realized it wasn't so much about being naked with her as much as it was about seeing her naked. Seeing a real-life, healthy woman in the nude, up close, personally, intimately, safely. But how would that work? Was it even worth whatever it was going to cost him?

He pulled away from her, allowing himself to touch her hair, and then her shoulder, which he noted later must have been dusted with glitter, as he found traces of it on his fingertips, and on his pants.

"I can't," he said. "It's been so long. I feel like I don't even know how anymore." Better to admit an alternate insecurity, he thought. The truth seemed much more humiliating. And anyway it was not a lie.

"You came all this way to stop now?" she said.

That challenge might have worked on a younger man, but not him. The fire in his loins was a particular kind. He was desperate, but he would not be rushed. He had not lived this long in life to be pushed around by a stranger.

"No, I think it's enough," he said.

"What about if I give you a hand?" said Tracy quietly.

He nodded, and she swept herself up and away, down the hall to the bathroom, returning shortly with two hand towels and a large pump bottle of lotion. She put the bottle of lotion next to the picture of her and Mitzi, one towel on her lap, and one towel on his. She kissed him again.

"Do you like to kiss?" she said. He nodded. She put her hand on his face and then ran it down his chest—quicker than he would have liked, and he could have said that and she would have listened, but he felt completely out of control and unable to speak—and straight to his crotch, where she rustled around softly—*It's right* there. *Good God, woman, how can you miss it?*—until she found what she was looking for. She petted him on the outside of his pants, and then quickly unbuttoned his pants, unzipped his fly, and then released his penis from his boxer shorts. She stroked it, and then stopped and leaned over to where the bottle of lotion sat. She pumped the bottle a few times. It was an anticellulite lotion, Middlestein noticed. She rubbed it on him.

"Do you like it this way?" she said. Her voice was girlish and flirty, and her eyes were direct. "I bet you like it this way." She didn't wait for a response, she surrounded him quickly—Listen, can you blame her? Ten-thirty on a Tuesday? Let's get a move on already, buddy—and it took not long until he came.

Middlestein felt great! He drove home fast. No traffic! Fantastic! He was thrilled, if only because he knew he was going to sleep like a rock that night. But for now he was still all jazzed up. He felt ten years younger. God, she was good. He was pretty sure he was never going to see her again—one hundred bucks for a handy?—but it was nice to have that number in his back pocket in case of an emotional emergency. She was clean and local, and he felt safe with her. Still he didn't know how comfortable he felt supporting, even in the smallest of ways, a woman who had more square footage than he did.

But it had been luxurious to be reminded of the pleasures of a woman's touch, the delicate thrill of its softness, the tension of trusting her to touch him the right way, the tiny death and rebirth that came with an orgasm. It wasn't soulful, necessarily, but it felt deep to Middlestein. He would renew his search for a woman.

He sat at his desk, white, long, clean, with a slight chip where he had banged the IKEA package against the wall of the lobby on his way in the door, turned on his computer, and selected the bookmark for the dating site for Jews. Forty was too young, he knew that now, he had known it all along, but now it had been confirmed. He wanted to take his clothes off with someone, but he needed to feel like the two of them were closer to equal. He changed his search parameters; now he was looking for women from fifty to sixty years of age.

And suddenly there were two hundred new results in the queue; a whole new world had opened up because Middlestein had decided to date age-appropriately. He clicked through a dozen of them until he found a picture of a dark, curly-haired woman, ample, smiling, appearing much younger than sixty, so familiar-looking that he was immediately attracted to her simply because he found familiarity, rare these days, so comforting. He opened her ad and realized he was staring at a picture of his wife, Edie, from ten years earlier, before they had fallen out of love with each other, before they had drifted so far apart it was as if they were on opposite ends of the world.

He knew when that photo was taken: It was on their trip to Italy. It was their first vacation together after Robin had gone away to college and then there was nothing left but the two of them. They were fifty years old. They had been raising children for the past twenty-five years. They should have been ready for their Part Two. He read about Part Two in magazines, he had heard about it from his friends. He wanted his Part Two.

But instead they had fought over everything, every detail. Or rather, she had fought with him, derided every suggestion he made. What did he know about Rome? She was the one who had studied Italian in college and spent two weeks in Italy after graduation. She was the one who had once been basically *fluent* in the language and would surely be again after a day or two there. Why would they go on a tour when they could walk the streets just fine on their own? Why would they stay at a hotel near the Vatican when it was so far away from everything else? Why, when they finally arrived there, had it not occurred to him to bring better shoes? (This was when his knees were just starting to go, he remembered, and that mile-long walk through the Vatican crushed him, and the minute he complained just once, she had snapped, so by the time they got to the Sistine Chapel, she was practically shrieking, and only the repeated shushing of the security guards had quieted her.) Why was he still jet-lagged? Why was he being so weird about taking the bus if he was complaining about walking? Why did he order the same thing every night? Why didn't he have an open mind? Why couldn't he just enjoy himself? That might have been the vacation that killed them, or it might have been the beginning of the end. It was hard to pinpoint it. He wondered if he was having a delayed reaction, by a decade. Here he was thinking it was everything, but instead maybe it was just that one moment in time.

When they got to the Trevi Fountain that day, he was limping, his hips, his ankles, his back, everything was shattered. Edie had already consumed five espressos and two gelatos, and he had wondered if she would ever sleep again. Some pleasant-enough American girl, a little older than Robin, a tourist like them, innocent to the doom she was witnessing, offered to take their picture with the fountain as the backdrop. The result was a photo of two people standing far apart, and he knew he was unsmiling in the other half of it, the half, he noticed, that Edie had cut out of the picture. What he saw online was just her, her handbag looped over her arm, that pretty silk dress that fell nicely around her wide, sexy hips, her hair a majestic throng of curls (it had rained that morning, and the air was still humid), still a reasonably good-looking woman with an intense, hopped-up-on-caffeine smile on her face. She looked like she was clever. She looked a little dangerous. Slightly past her prime, but still she seemed ripe. If he didn't know her, he would have thought she was fascinating. If he didn't know her, he would have thought she was just his type. *I want that woman back,* he thought. *I want that woman, but I want her to still love me.* And he knew now—he had known this for a long time, but he had sealed it with every decision he had made in the last two months—that she was never going to love him again.

Edie, 210 Pounds

HERE IS WHAT was on the tray: one Big Mac, one large fries, two Happy Meals, one McRib sandwich (because it was a new sandwich, and how often did a new sandwich come along?), one Diet Coke, two orange juices, one chocolate shake, one apple pie for everyone to share, and three chocolate chip cookies, one for Edie, one for little Robin, and one for Benny, who was getting to be such a big boy now. Edie would definitely eat the Big Mac and the McRib sandwich all on her own, although she had asked Benny if he had wanted to try it, pointing to the cardboard advertisement dangling from the ceiling like a mobile over a baby's crib, and he had nodded yes. She had also asked him if he wanted a chocolate chip cookie, sitting there looking so moist and chewy in its plastic display case, or an apple pie, he could have either, and he said, "Neither," and she had said, "Well, maybe we should get both just in case," and he had shrugged. It was all the same to him; around his house nothing ever went to waste (which meant everything got eaten by someone in the end), and also he was only just six years old and didn't have strong opinions one way or another about much of anything, or at least not about food, because, after all, it was just food.

What was food to a six-year-old? Sometimes Benny would eat only the same thing for weeks at a time (macaroni and cheese for most of the winter; turkey sandwiches, sometimes minus the turkey and sometimes minus the bread, for all of March), and Edie didn't have the energy to argue with him. It was not about taste. It was about some sort of affection or association with a memory, she suspected. Like, maybe she had given him macaroni and cheese on the first cold day of the year and it had warmed him up so beautifully that he craved that same sensation on repeat. Perhaps there was a favorite cartoon character of his who loved turkey sandwiches. Or a Muppet? It had nothing to do with his innocent young palate. He could not be expected to be excited about the new McRib sandwich. It was meaningless to him.

Edie was saving the McRib for last, because it was a treat, almost like a dessert sandwich. She had already finished her fries, decimated them moments after the three of them had sat down, and was working on Benny's bag, while Benny, in a thoughtful and organized manner, plucked apart the free plastic toy that had come with his meal. Robin was happily banging the hell out of her own toy until Edie finally retrieved it from her just to stop all the noise.

Big Mac-wise, she had this new habit of picking

out the middle layer of bun from her sandwich, because she had heard the one time she went to Weight Watchers that half the battle was the bread. She would even have eaten the McRib minus the roll entirely, only obviously that would have made a huge mess. Best to eat it as intended. She took a bite of the Big Mac and considered it without the extra slice of bun, which lay nearby covered in flecks of lettuce and salmon-pink special sauce. There was literally no impact on the taste, and yet there was something missing in the experience, an extra layer of spongy pleasure.

Holy cow, she was thinking a lot about food.

She was so tired from her day, and so happy to not have to think about work (although she did not mind her job; she had never minded putting in a hard day's work, it was, in her opinion, as she had been raised to believe, both an extremely Jewish and American way to behave, being a good worker was), and *in theory,* she should be happy to spend time with her children, but sometimes she found them a little dull. Playing with them was boring, and it wasn't even their fault. It was just the notion of playing itself. She had never gotten the hang of it, even when she was a child. You needed to be able to adopt a personality other than your own in order to fully immerse yourself in the world of play, and it was burden enough carrying her own self around.

"Don't you guys have anything of interest to

say?" she said in the direction of her children. It didn't matter which one answered. "What did you do today?"

Benny looked up from the pile of plastic parts. Minutes ago it had been an airplane. Now it was waste.

"I went to school," he said.

"Did you learn anything?" she said. One-two-three bites, and the Big Mac was finished.

"We counted a lot today," he said. "There was a lot of counting, and I played catch during recess with three different boys and one girl. Craig, Eric, Russell, and Lea, and then Lea got hit in the head and we had to stop playing. And I made this." He pulled from his pocket a string of orange and pink beads on a long, narrow rubber thread and held it up in the air. "It's for you." He smiled—oh, he beamed! The beam that could break your heart.

I'm a shit, thought Edie.

"It is the most beautiful necklace I have ever seen in my entire life," she said. She took it from his tiny hand and then tied it around her neck.

"You look pretty," he said.

She did not look pretty, she thought. She did not believe she had looked pretty in a long time. Her business clothes no longer fit her right, not her jackets, not her shirts, not her skirts, not her pants, not her pantyhose, not even her shoes—or rather, she no longer fit them right—but she could not bring herself to buy a new wardrobe. Maybe if she gave Weight Watchers a shot this time. There was always the vague promise of that lingering in her future.

"What about you?" she said to Robin.

Robin spent her mornings in a day-care center at the JCC and her afternoons in the backyard of a young woman who lived one town over, along with two other toddlers, the parents of whom worked as lawyers with Edie at the firm. The baby-sitter, barely twenty years old if that, was supposedly the widow of a cousin of a senior partner, but Edie was almost certain she was his mistress. She was an Italian girl, this Tracy, from Elmwood Park originally, and had no real explanation for why she was now suddenly living in the suburbs. And there were no pictures up in her home, no past, no history, just fresh-bought furniture and a small, fancy, yapping dog. "A bichon frisé," Tracy had slurred proudly, as if she were fluent in French. Edie had no complaints about the woman; she seemed to genuinely like the children, even enjoyed playing with them, liked to get down on her hands and knees and crawl around in the dirt with them, her plump yet still somehow tiny behind in the air. Wagging it like a dog. The dog barking next to her. The kids barking. Everyone pretending to be a dog. All the working mothers standing there in the suburbs laughing at the too-loud, thick-Chicago-accented but still extremely hot Italian tomato rolling around in the dirt with their three brilliant babies.

Edie didn't even know whether she would ever be able to get back up again if she dropped down that low to the earth.

"Strawberry," said Robin.

"You ate a strawberry," said Edie. "You like strawberries." She said this as if she were suddenly realizing this detail about her child for the first time.

Robin nodded.

"You like fries?" said Edie. She pushed the tiny white paper packet of fries that had been residing in her daughter's Happy Meal box toward her. "If you're not going to eat them, I will."

"I like fries," said Robin.

Edie took two of them from the packet, and then Robin pulled it back toward her, covering it with her hands. "Mine!" she said.

"Just give me a couple more," said Edie.

"No. Mine," Robin said.

Once Edie had been something close to an intellectual, and she took great joy in using her brain to its fullest, the first moments of the day in particular a blissful time to think big thoughts. Now she was arguing with a two-year-old about french fries. Around the dinner table, her parents, now deceased, her mother before her father, but he soon after—he should have lived longer, he *could* have, but he crumpled without his beloved, no matter how much Edie begged for him to try to live for her sake—spoke of ideas and ideals, wondering with hope what it would take to make all the citizens of the world fit together in their own unique ways. Once she'd lived in a home that had bookshelves filled with novels written in Russian; her parents' collection was now trapped in taped-up boxes in Richard and Edie's crawl space. She had lost her way. Her father had spent much of his spare time quietly helping immigrants set up new lives for themselves in the suburbs of Chicago. She worked for a law firm that worked almost exclusively for corporations developing shopping plazas all along Dundee Road, from I-94 to Route 53 to beyond, and when they were done with that road, they would probably find another one.

Thirty years old, and she had failed. Look at the rubble, the empty fast-food wrappers, the mashed-up plastic toy parts. She had no idea what her ass looked like anymore; it had been so long since she'd dared look in a mirror. Edie, Edie, Edie.

She had a husband. He existed. He had opened a pharmacy with the help of much of her inheritance, an impressive stash of Israeli bonds her father had purchased over the years, his fervid support of the country traded for another dream. (That the money was never to return to her was barely mentioned, then ignored, and finally actively forgotten to the point where the truth disappeared entirely.) He toiled at the pharmacy from before she woke up in the morning till long after she had picked up the children from day care. Often his appearances at dinner felt like something from an up-and-coming comedian on *The Tonight Show*. He would walk in at the end of the meal, grinning, his children dousing him with noisy attention, and then tell the best story from his day. Edie would stare at him, glazed, uncertain if what he was saying was truly entertaining or not. Sometimes she laughed. Sometimes it was just easier to laugh.

Richard had no problem playing with the children. He had to engage in real conversations with people all day long, and Edie suspected he was secretly a little misanthropic. He had, after all, chosen a profession where there was an entire counter between him and the people he served, a line that could never be crossed. But the kids, these miniature versions of themselves, especially Benny, his boy, for him, were exactly what he needed at the end of the day. They didn't talk back or question him; they weren't deliverymen, again with the wrong order, or batty old neighborhood women demanding a discount; they didn't shoplift, nor did they ask for credit. They crawled all over him, whispering sweet nonsense in his ear. Neither Edie nor Robin knew yet that when the kids grew older and began having ideas and opinions at odds with Richard's he would shut them out of his affections with such carelessness.

(*But this is when things get interesting,* Edie would think as he stormed out of the room again, after an argument with fourteen-year-old Robin. Never mind him. Robin would just have to love her mother best.)

"Fine, take the fries," she said to her daughter.

She cracked open the McRib box and eyed the dark red, sticky sandwich. Suddenly she felt like an animal; she wanted to drag the sandwich somewhere, not anywhere in this McDonald's, not a booth, not Playland, but to a park, a shrouded corner of woods underneath shimmering tree branches, green, dark, and serene, and then, when she was certain she was completely alone, she wanted to tear that sandwich apart with her teeth. But she couldn't just leave her children there, could she? You didn't need to be a graduate of Northwestern Law to know that that was illegal.

And then, finally, there was her husband coming through the door, wrinkling his nose at the assault of that particular McDonald's smell (which Edie loved, so much hope in that grilled, salty, sweet, meaty air), striding over to the table with his last burst of energy for the day, which he had reserved solely for his children and only a little bit for his wife. He scanned quickly the detritus of the table, the damage that had been done by Edie, and then slid in next to Benny, who threw his arms around his waist. Richard picked up the McRib box—the sandwich still untouched—and peered into it.

"Can I have this?" he said.

"I was going to eat it," she said.

He leaned over Robin in her high chair and kissed her curly-haired head, then took one of her fries. Robin said, "Mine," and Richard said, "What's mine is yours, kid."

"You're twenty minutes late," said Edie.

"Traffic," said Richard.

"Give me a break with the traffic," said Edie. "You work less than a mile away."

"Do you want to go look outside and see?" he said. "Bumper to bumper."

"I hate you," Edie said in a peaceful-sounding voice. Did Benny know what that word meant yet? What it meant to hate?

"Well then, it must be a Thursday," said Richard cheerfully. "Benny, look at what you did here." He fished through the detached plane parts. "I need to eat something, wife. I really can't have that?"

"No, you can't have that," said Edie, no longer peaceful, now spitting. "Twenty minutes ago is when we ordered our meal. An hour ago is when I picked them up from day care. Ninety minutes ago is when I got off work. Ten hours ago is when I dropped them off—"

"Hey, I have an idea," said Richard.

"You have so many wonderful ideas," said Edie.

"Why don't I take these kids over to the Playland and you sit here by yourself for five minutes and eat your sandwich?"

"I don't even want to sit here," she said. She suddenly didn't want to be reminded of what she had eaten, the wrappers, the garbage, the junk.

"So sit somewhere else," he said. "I don't care where you sit. Anyone care where your mother sits?"

No one cared where their mother sat.

She walked to the far corner of the restaurant, to the booth closest to the bathroom, where no one ever sat but the employees on break, looking back only once at her husband gathering up the children; he gave her a nod, and that was it. She sat down with her McRib sandwich and then started shivering, because it was suddenly cold in the restaurant, away from the mess, the heat of her family, the source of her frustration. She pulled out the newspaper from her purse. Edie took a bite of her McRib and flattened out the front page. Was this really happening to her? Because this was perfection.

This happened a lot in the future, in their family, in their lives, going out to dinner with Edie sitting at a separate table. For years this went on, until they all stopped eating together entirely, Benny and Robin growing up thinking it was something everyone did, and not realizing that it wasn't until it didn't matter anymore anyway. As an adult, Robin found herself behaving exactly the same as her mother without even knowing it, always alone at meals, eating, reading, alone, while Benny married young and his doting wife, at home with the kids, had a hot, non-fast-food-related meal on the table every night. In the end it was not the worst thing that had happened to them in their lives. "It could have been much, much worse," Benny said to his sister at their mother's funeral, and she could not argue. "They could have starved us," said Robin. "They could have beat us," said Benny. It was a game they could play for hours.

The day Edie dined alone with her McRib sandwich was the one-year anniversary of the Mount St. Helens eruption. It had made the front page, even though it happened in another state. Tragedy ripens in memory. Fifty-seven people had died. They believed that the mountain was their friend. They didn't want to leave their homes behind. Who would they be without their homes?

What fools, thought Edie. *I'd run like hell if I could.*

Exodus

AFTER THIRTEEN SUCCESSFUL years of rejecting Judaism—this included no High Holidays with her parents, no bar mitzvahs of distant relations, no hanging out at the Hillel House in college, no Purim, no Passover, no Shabbat, no nothing except for Hanukkah at her brother's house, which got a pass because gifts were exchanged, and also because her niece and nephew, both of whom she was fond of, had always enjoyed that holiday so much—Robin wasn't exactly sure how she had ended up at this crowded seder, but there she was, in her trim blue dress, holding her I-guess-he's-my-boyfriend's hand in his parents' living room in Northbrook, Illinois. She had instinctively grabbed it, because otherwise she thought she might have been swept away in the crowd of people. She wasn't trying to be cute or affectionate; she was just trying to save her life.

"I don't get why you hate it so much," he had said.

This was a few weeks before Passover, when he had first asked her to come with him, to eat a good meal, to relax, to meet his family. It was important to him. She could tell this because he wasn't letting it drop, and, up until recently, he had been letting everything drop all the time with her. They drank when she wanted to drink; they had sex when she wanted to have sex. The sex, by the way, was the best both had had in their lives, the true notion of coupling finally revealed to the two of them at least physically, the way they curled up into each other, sweaty, salty, lustful messes, alternating their dialogue between dirty and dizzyingly sweet talk. But out of the bed they didn't talk about their future together; they spoke mainly about her sick mother, her asshole dad, how her day had been, sometimes how his day had been, and that was it. Occasionally she said something like, "My parents are so crazy I swear they're going to drive me to therapy," and he would say, "Do you feel like you want to go to therapy?" and she would say, "Are you saying I need therapy?" and he would raise his hands in the air and walk away rather than answer that question, no fool was he. She was completely running the show. But when she said no to the dinner, that it wasn't her scene, he jerked back his head, his soft, blond, fuzzy, gentle head, and gave her a fixed look.

"Me and Judaism, we don't get along," she said.

"It's a family dinner," he said. "With just a touch of Jew."

"Please," she said. "Don't make me."

"I'm the one saying please," he said. "You're the one saying no."

She crushed herself into a ball on his couch, knees up, arms around her legs, head against her knees.

"Why is this so hard for you, to just say yes? It's a dinner, a really good dinner, with some nice people. It's not a big deal."

"If it's not a big deal, then why do I have to go?" she said.

Daniel sat next to her on the couch, and, in a shocking display of spine, put his face next to hers and said, "What is this really about?"

Robin weaved through Daniel's parents' home warily, attached to his fingertips. It was his home, too, she supposed; he had grown up there, after all. Even though he had gone to college, lived in San Francisco for five years, six months in New York on a freelance project, Austin, San Francisco, and then finally in Chicago, where he lived happily, quietly, contentedly (why was he so content? what was his secret?), in the apartment beneath hers. Of all those places, all those different apartments, all those different *homes,* this was the place he talked about the most fondly, the most easily, so when he said, "I'm going home for the weekend," she knew exactly where he meant.

Everyone else felt right at home there, too. There were bodies stretched everywhere, on couches, on chairs, small children splayed on the floor with coloring books and boxes of crayons. (This last part Robin approved of as a teacher, none of those bleeping-blooping toys that were destroying America and contributing to noise pollution. She loved her iPhone as much as the next thirty-year-old with a small disposable income, but for children she felt strongly that imagination should still be enough, and it never was anymore.) She met Daniel's two brothers and one sister, a few nieces and nephews, six cousins of various ages, two sets of aunts and uncles, his lone living grandfather, two former next-door neighbors who had moved to Florida but came back a few times a year, who were *like family,* his mother, his father, and a great-aunt Faye and her friend Naomi, who both sat the entire night in a small alcove in the kitchen barking orders at Daniel's mother.

"You better check the brisket," Faye was saying as Daniel and Robin walked into the kitchen. Daniel's mother, a bustling, tender-eyed woman Robin's mother's age, sighed not quite imperceptibly, then unscrewed a bottle of Manischewitz and placed it next to several other open bottles. She had everything under control, even if Faye didn't think so; foil-covered dishes of food were organized neatly on countertops.

"Why don't you check the brisket if you know so much?" said Naomi.

"All right, I'll check the brisket," said Faye.

"It's fine," said Daniel's mother.

"You don't know anything about anything," said Faye. She shuffled across the kitchen to the oven, opened it, and peered inside. "It needs a little more time," she concluded.

"I know it needs a little more time," said Daniel's mother. "I know when I'm supposed to take it out of the oven."

"I'm starving," Faye said to Naomi. "Are you starving?"

"Starving," said Naomi.

"You could have started sooner," said Faye. Robin noticed she had the hint of an Eastern European accent. She sat back down, then spotted Daniel and Robin. "Daniel, come here and give me a kiss. This one, too." She pointed at Robin. "Come here." Daniel hugged his great-aunt, and then Robin leaned in and hugged her also. She was a tiny collection of bones, almost childlike in her frame, and she smelled strongly of Chanel No. 5. She wore diamonds in her ears and around her neck and on several of her fingers, and her hair glittered white. "Look at this," she said. She patted Robin on the face, her hands gentle. "Look what Daniel found."

"Well, if you really want to know," Robin said, flustered, miserable. There were issues being forced all over the place lately, and it had been his fault, he knew it. He was pushing the two of them forward, as a couple, an entity. He had decided she was the one for him. He had never met anyone before who needed him like she did, even if she couldn't admit it.

"I really want to know," he said. He leaned back and put his arm around her, she unfolded herself into him, and then she began to speak.

"I hated Hebrew school," she said.

"Was there someone who liked Hebrew school?" he said.

"All the other kids went to the same grammar school and junior high school and summer camp, and they saw each other every day, all day long, and were all best friends with each other. And I was this interloper. Plus, I was fat, did I ever tell you I was a fat kid?"

Yes, she had told him she was fat.

"Everyone made fun of me. The girls were the worst, those bitchy little princesses," she said. "It was two hours of hell, three times a week, for years. How many years? Like five years."

Robin's eyes narrowed and her cheeks grew pinched, and it made Daniel love her less in that moment. Those faces she made never did her any favors, but there was no way to actually tell her that. You had to take the good with the bad: that was how Daniel felt. Later on, when her arms were wrapped around his back and her fingers were in his hair, the way she stroked his face, the kisses she laid on his neck, he wouldn't be thinking about that weird squint she had when she was pissed off.

"I'm sympathetic to your pain, but that's not enough of a reason to reject religion outright," he said. "We all had a lot of pain growing up."

Daniel had been a boy genius, and then a teen genius. (Though now as an adult, after a dozen years of drinking and a long-standing romance with Adderall that had ended only in the last year, he was probably just pretty smart.) He wasn't sure why being smart necessitated being tortured by his classmates. He remembered in particular a football player who sat behind him in Spanish class sophomore year, who at least once a day stabbed him in the back of the head with a pencil until one day his barber discovered a dripping green hole there and he was rushed to the emergency room, and there were shots, the whole nine, and when he returned to school the next week, he found that the seating chart had been reorganized and he had been moved to a corner by himself, which, as he looked back now, should have bothered him, but at the time it just gave him a giant sense of relief.

Still, he never complained about it, because he now made a living off the thing that was once a source of his pain. He also knew that the football player, husky, yellowing, was now a waiter at the McCormick & Schmick's at Old Orchard—Daniel had seen him last year while holiday shopping with his mother—and even though he had never thought that he needed any resolution in his life of those dark years, that did not make the moment any less sweet. In fact, it might have been the air-conditioning in the mall, but he was pretty sure he had tingled.

Robin started to say something that seemed like it was going to be important: the deep inhale, the bunched-up fists, the grim set to her mouth. But instead she simply said, "I just felt like it got shoved down my throat."

His girlfriend was making excuses. Maybe he'd hear the real story later, and maybe he wouldn't, though he suspected he would. There was so much dramatic tension built up all over her, in every tight cell of her body, and he loved watching it unfold. Whatever emotions she was experiencing—and they were not entirely bad; in fact, they were sometimes so delicate and passionate that it was as if he could see right through to her soul—she made it count. On a daily basis, she took great big gulps of feelings, and whatever was left over she would pass on to him. All that Adderall had taken its toll on Daniel: It was simply harder to feel things now, so he would grab sensations when he could get them. Being with Robin was like being stabbed with a million pinpricks at once. He was shocked by how good that felt.

"I'm sure it was awful," he said.

"You don't even know the half of it," she whimpered.

"It sounds like something you should talk about in therapy, if you ever decide to go to therapy," he said.

She began to protest, but he had already had this discussion with her. It was not *her* problem, of course. It was *theirs*. He already knew how to finish the sentence.

"Not that I'm telling you you need to go to therapy," he continued. "Because I'm not. But in the meantime, I think you can come have dinner with my family."

There was a small card table set up in the living room and then a longer table next to that and then another long table in the foyer between the living room and the dining room, and then finally there was the long, gorgeous oak dining room table, and all of Daniel's family members were distributed among these tables, the children at one table, the adult children at the next table, the parents of both groups of children at the next. Both rooms smelled intensely of brisket. Except for the children, who dined on plastic, everyone had matching silverware and plates and wineglasses, and the tables were beautiful, they shimmered flawlessly in the candlelight. At every place setting there was a printout of a Haggadah, and a green rubber frog finger puppet. Robin put one on her pinkie and waved it at Daniel.

"They're supposed to represent the plague," he said to her. She stretched her memory, and recalled that it was something to do with the Exodus; she had blocked it all out so long ago.

"What happened to the fancy Haggadahs?" yelled a cousin from the living room. It was the only way anyone could hear anyone else from one room to the other.

"Those were gorgeous," said another.

"There was a flood in the basement," said Daniel's father.

"Why were they in the basement?" asked Faye, from the kitchen.

"I don't even want to talk about it," said his mother quietly.

Robin liked Daniel's mother, whom she had met before, when Daniel was just the downstairs neighbor she got drunk with during happy hour on Fridays (and also sometimes on Sundays during brunch, and obviously on Thursdays, too, because she would never make it through Friday without going out on Thursday night), and meeting his family was no big deal. His mother had worked for many years in the public-school system as a librarian and then had gone back to graduate school and had worked her way up at Northwestern, where she now taught library science. Robin admired her ambition and envied her placidity. It was one of the things she liked most in Daniel, too: his calm. If she were forced to detail the things she liked about Daniel, that quality would have been on the list.

The Manischewitz was so sweet that even Robin couldn't drink it, and so she left the glass untouched except for those few sips required by Jewish law.

"Got anything else?" said Daniel. He was ready for any reason she threw at him as to why she would not be attending his family's seder. For once he had found a battle worth fighting.

She couldn't bring herself to mention that she felt like she would be cheating on her family with his family if she spent the holiday with them. Her brother and his wife had been inviting her to their house for Passover since she had moved back from New York, and she had said no for eight years straight. From her parents—when they were still together; they had split a few months before—she got the pre–High Holiday invitation ("It would make your father so happy to see you there," her mother would say) as well as the post–High Holiday guilt trip ("Would it have killed you to do something to make your mother happy?" her father would say). The one-two punch. Coming and going. She wished she could have helped them all feel a little bit better about their universe, but she was certain that the hours spent with them, head bowed in prayer, would have been excruciating.

But she had been spending enough time with her family lately, or at least with her newly single mother. Her sister-in-law, Rachelle, had devised all these plans to help her mother, her obese, diabetes-stricken, heartbroken mother, lose weight and get in shape, and had sent Robin an e-mail detailing how if they were all on the same team and worked together and abided by this schedule, Monday to Saturday, then there would be hope, there was still hope, and could Robin please take Saturdays, if she would just take Saturdays, Rachelle would do the rest. And so Robin had been coming into the suburbs once a week, and she and her mother had been doing as instructed, taking a mile-long walk together around the high-school track, Edie huffing and limping, though suffering silently otherwise, unwilling to admit that this was totally abnormal, that she and her daughter had never in their lives gone for a mile-long walk together, let alone on the high-school track, but if they admitted how weird it was, then they would have to admit everything else about her health, and neither one of them wanted to talk about that, because they were both completely terrified for different reasons, and for the same reasons also.

Afterward they would get drunk together in Edie's kitchen, in a really aggressive and committed fashion. Their drinking was no joke: a bottle each in two hours. They poured and drank, and Edie spoke. *Let me tell you a little something about your father,* she would say. *Oh, I've got a story for you.* She would stumble over her words. *You want to know the real truth?*

If you only knew.

Now Robin knew everything.

Then she would take the train back to the city drunk, but instead of going home, up just one more flight of stairs, she'd go to Daniel's apartment, with all his computer monitors and his photographs and his cookbooks that he never even needed to open anymore because he had his favorite recipes memorized. And sometimes they would talk, or sometimes she would put her hand on his mouth and she would say *please* and he would say *okay* and they would just go to sleep, and when they woke up, he would just rest himself in her, slightly hard, and not move at all, except for every so often just to keep himself hard, and he would whisper, "We don't have to do anything at all but just be." Sometimes she would just lie on the couch and stare at the ceiling, a corpse, and he would sit in the corner and strum his guitar, old indie-rock songs she kind of knew the words to. Sometimes they would go across to the dive bar—their bar now—and get even drunker and come back to his place and have sometimes painful but emotionally necessary sex, and she could barely look at him afterward, even though he never took his eyes off her for a second.

I always feel like you're waiting for me to say something, she told him once in her head, where it was safe for sentences like that.

Daniel was still waiting for her to give him another reason she couldn't go to dinner, and she had run out of reasons. "Can I bring anything?" she asked, because her mother had raised her right.

After the Four Questions (asked, with great sincerity, by Daniel's youngest cousin, Ashley, a nine-year-old girl with a booming voice), after the Plagues (Daniel's father, earnest, blocky, bushy-browed, dipping his finger dramatically into his wineglass), after a noisy rendition of "Dayenu" (to which Robin found herself quickly remembering the words), after the gefilte fish and the matzo-ball soup and the brisket and the chicken and the chocolate-covered matzo and the caramel-covered matzo and the honey nut cake (all of which Robin ate too much of, which made her feel guilty and bad and then sad), there was the slow exit, everyone jamming themselves into coats, negotiations, good-byes, promises, wishes, dreams. A crowd of Jews trying to get home.

Who would drive Danny and his girlfriend to the train station? What a pleasure you are. How nice to see your face around here.

I'm not his girlfriend, she wanted to say.

When Robin saw two stray dishes on the dining-room table, an escape plan quickly formed, and she slid into the kitchen. Dishes, she could do dishes until it was time to leave. Daniel's mother was in there, yelling at his father.

"All night I had to listen to her complain," she snapped. "I cannot tolerate another second. Just fucking drive her home. She's your aunt, not mine."

They both looked up, reflexive smiles skimming momentarily across their faces, ripples across a pond. They were too tired to pretend that it had been anything less than an extremely long night.

"Dishes," said Robin, and she lamely held up the cake-stained plates. Daniel's mother took them from her. "It was a very nice night," Robin said.

"You are welcome in our home anytime," said his mother.

"I'll give you a ride to the train station," said his father.

Somehow, he had conned her into this night with his family even though she was certain she had been trying to keep an emotional distance between herself and Daniel for months, since that first night they were together when she had whispered in his ear, "This doesn't mean anything." He had said nothing in return, which she took as an agreement, or at least an admission of acceptance.

He was her neighbor, he was her friend, and she did care about him, but she never wanted to be in a relationship ever again. Because relationships were the worst. So many obligations. So many compromises. So many arguments. Someone always got destroyed in the end. Sometimes everyone got destroyed in the end.

They weren't the only people returning to the city from suburban seders that night, but they ignored them and slunk down in their seats. Daniel reached into his pocket and pulled out two of the rubber frog finger puppets, took Robin's hand, and put one on her pinkie, then put one on his own. He banged the head of one frog against the other.

"I walked in on your parents arguing in the kitchen," she said.

He shrugged and said, "Sometimes they don't agree."

"It was shocking."

"Not all fighting leads to divorce," he said. He pulled the frog off his finger and looked out the window.

"You're an expert now?" she said. Suddenly everything about her was out of control: She wasn't saying what she meant, her heart felt hot, her limbs were loose.

"Have you considered the possibility that your parents are better off without each other?"

Only every day since her mother had told her that her father was gone.

"Never," she said, red-faced, sweaty, bloated with untruths. She had eaten too much of his mother's brisket. She had a Tupperware container of it sitting in her lap that she planned on dumping out the moment she got home. Maybe she would dump him out along with it.

"Look, everything was fine up until then. It wasn't an all-bad night, right?" He poked her. "Being Jewish for a night isn't completely terrible."

"I tuned a lot of it out," she said.

"What is wrong with you?" he said. "How can you possibly hate it?"

"I don't hate it," she said. "It just seems to me like if you're going to utter those words, be devoted and present and worshipful, be committed, then you should really believe in it. Really love it. And I don't get why I should love it. Why it's the right way and everything else is the wrong way. I never understood."

"It doesn't have to be that complicated," he said. "You could just participate in order to feel connected to something bigger than yourself. It makes me feel safe. Not alone."

"That's what your friends are for," she said.

"Sometimes friends aren't enough," he said.

"I remain unconvinced," she said. *We are going to argue about this for eternity,* she thought.

"Can you just stop being so tough for a minute?" he said.

"No," she said.

And would you hate her if she started to cry? Did she have you convinced that she really was that tough? Would you find her weak, a weak, pathetic girl, crying because she was losing an argument, losing herself, losing herself into him, and she hadn't let herself feel that way in so long? Would you still want to know her, could you still respect her, if she was the kind of girl who cried when she realized she was falling in love?

Edie, 241 Pounds

THE LETTER WENT out on a Friday, but Edie already knew what it was going to say. Her daughter, Robin, flipped it miserably in front of her at the kitchen table, where Edie had collapsed after arriving home from work, her hand resting on an unopened package of fat-free (top ingredient: sugar) cookies. She messily ripped the edge of the delicate plastic wrapping with her fingertips, leaving a jagged opening down the middle of the package, so instead of just one row of dark, spongy, devil's-food-cake cookies, there were two, and, with the slightest tug of her index finger and thumb, all three were revealed. There they all were. Waiting. The cookies smelled like nothing, like air, and that's how they felt inside her, too. They never filled her up, no matter how many she ate. Once, at night, when she was certain everyone was in bed, she had eaten two boxes of the cookies, just to see what would happen, and it had done nothing to her. Edie couldn't feel a thing.

She pushed the package toward her daughter, who got up from the end of the table and took half of one row of cookies into her hands, then returned to face her mother down at the end of the long table. Six cookies. Fat-free.

"This looks important," said her mother.

Her daughter looked up at her, eyes stark and serious and red-rimmed, half a cookie sticking from her mouth like a helpless mouse captured by a sharp house cat. She looked just as her mother had at her age, plump, fresh-faced, though she carried the weight differently because she was shorter than her mother, so perhaps she was a little wider around the hips. She took the rest of the cookie into her mouth with just her tongue. She hadn't spoken to her mother in two days, because her mother hadn't allowed her to go to the hospital when she had wanted to, and then it was too late, and now all that was left was this letter.

It was from the high school; Robin had already opened it, read it, and shoved it back into the envelope, so Edie just shook out the paper with one hand while holding a cookie with the other. Her daughter had already eaten all her cookies and was reaching for more.

A boy had killed himself, that's what the letter said. Another one was in a mental hospital. (That part wasn't mentioned in the letter, but Edie had heard this from the school guidance counselor when he had called her at work that afternoon.) The weekend before, the two boys and her daughter had driven downtown to see the Smashing Pumpkins play at a festival, and Robin had returned home drunk and Edie had let it slide because Robin was actually a good little drunk:

she did not have much of a hangover, no moaning the next day, and Edie hadn't had to hold her hair back over the toilet like she did for several roommates of hers in college. She was simply giggly, and she raved about the show, and she didn't appear to have been molested in any way. Maybe Edie should have imparted some parental wisdom about alcohol at that moment, but she was in no position to be giving anyone advice about what they should or shouldn't consume.

They felt close, which they had been for Robin's entire life, especially in that period after her brother, Benny, went away to Champaign for college and the house had become extremely empty, her husband, Richard, always struggling to keep his three pharmacies afloat, engaging in some sort of pyramid scheme among businesses, driving back and forth between them, always hustling (she had to give him credit for that), even as he was failing. Edie and Robin were left behind with each other, and they joined forces at the kitchen table, Edie sharing (sometimes age-inappropriate) stories about her day, like the ones about her co-workers at the law firm, who were always more interesting than their job descriptions would suggest; they were office-supply thieves and part-time jazz musicians and heavy drinkers and cancer survivors. Or about the woman in line at the grocery store who had too many babies and a low-cut blouse and what seemed like a hundred coupons, and *why were they all for cat food?* And there was always something to say about family members, distant cousins who were getting divorces, because she had known all along *it was never going to last,* or wistful stories about family members who came over from Russia before the war, or directly after, because *it's important to know where you came from.* Together they sat, a haul of groceries in front of them, the prepackaged snacks one of their shared great delights in life.

Then Edie would send her daughter off to do her homework while she prepared their official dinner, something of real substance, steak or chicken or pasta. The pretense of all-together time at dinner had long faded, of course, with Richard showing up late for dinner or not at all. Edie never bothered to set a place for him. Sometimes Robin ate in her room, and that was fine with Edie. It felt good to be alone with your food, she understood. Even if the rhythm in their lives was a strange one, it was a rhythm nonetheless.

Then Robin started high school six months ago and became friends with these two boys, the dead one, and the one who was now locked away, and she had begun to disappear from Edie. Home late sometimes, or leaving after dinner. Phone calls late at night. The music coming from her bedroom grew louder for weeks, and then quieter, and it was almost as if there were no music at all. Edie stood in the hallway, holding in her breath, her ear pressed against the door to her daughter's bedroom. There was definitely something playing on her stereo. What kind of music was her daughter listening to these days? Edie used to know everything about her, and now she couldn't answer that question. She was embarrassed as much as worried.

And now she realized she knew nothing about her daughter at all. This boy had overdosed on pills. The letter didn't say that, but she had read about it in the newspaper, and the guidance counselor had confirmed it again that day. He had held on for two days, and her daughter had begged to go to the hospital, and she had said no because if it were Robin lying there (God forbid. Oy. *God forbid.*), Edie wouldn't want anyone else but family with her. And also she didn't want Robin anywhere near that kind of sickness. This wasn't like keeping her away from Benny for a week when he had the chicken pox in sixth grade. This was like Edie was two steps away from marching into that bedroom and rummaging through all her daughter's possessions to see what she was hiding, and hell no, her daughter was not going to hang out in the ICU of a hospital with the family of a boy who had just overdosed on pills.

"I'm sorry your friend died," said Edie.

Robin took another handful of cookies and continued her methodical quest for the decimation of all of fat-free-based-snack America.

On the wall across from the kitchen table hung a macramé owl with large brown agate stones for eyes. Edie had put it there when they moved into the house in 1980, when Robin was just a baby. The cleaning woman dusted it every week, but it still seemed to be coated with some sort of old filth. A twig hung forlornly from its claws. For ten years Edie had been meaning to take it down. No joke, an entire decade. But Edie had been busy. First it had just been pro bono consultation, anything to take her mind off the banalities of her suburban existence. But then the purpose of her volunteerism came into sharp focus in 1988, when Dukakis—married to a Jewish girl!—ran for office, and her old college roommate Carly, one of the top Democratic fund-raisers in Chicago, called and asked for her help. Edie had sent in a check, and made some phone calls to some of her friends, the Cohns and the Grodsteins and the Weinmans and the Frankens, all lovely people, and before she knew it, she was making phone calls to people she didn't know, and she discovered she was good at it. Paperwork and phone calls. She was most confident doing things where she could hide, where she didn't notice people noticing how heavy she had gotten. She could see it even in the eyes of her co-workers. But here was a way she could help. Here was a way she could make a difference. Carly didn't realize it, and Edie didn't know if she could ever properly communicate it to her, but she was pretty sure Carly had saved her life. So who had time to worry about wall hangings when there were Republicans to kick out of office?

But the boys? Who were these boys? She should have been worried. She had met them, but she hadn't paid enough attention. One was tall and thin and had longish (but seemingly clean) hair, and the other was short and a little stocky and had a shaved head. Both wore flannel shirts over white T-shirts and jeans with holes in the knees and Converse high-tops. They didn't smell like smoke, their pupils weren't dilated. They spoke little, and always smiled at her when she answered the door. They were always happy to see Robin. They both gave her high fives. They looked Jewish. Ethan and Aaron, Aaron and Ethan. How was she supposed to remember which was which?

Robin screamed at her the entire evening the boy went to the hospital, pleading, then demanding, that Edie let her go visit him. On her knees in the living room, with Richard sitting on the stairs, his presence pointless as usual, his elbows on his thighs, his chin in his hands, contributing absolutely nothing to the conversation. "She never listens to me anyway," is all he said. Worst parent on the planet. All he knew how to do was bark orders and walk away. He didn't understand that his daughter was smarter than that, that she wasn't a dog. And Edie thought she knew how to handle

Robin perfectly, but this, this hysterical girl, all Edie could do was try to hold her. When Robin was a toddler and she wasn't getting what she wanted, she used to hold her breath until she turned blue. Edie had always ignored those antics, until once she passed out, and Edie never ignored her again, but Robin never held her breath again either. Both of them had learned. But here she was, unleashed, uncontrolled. She was not blue, though. She was bright red.

"It's not our place," said Edie. "He needs his family."

"I'm one of his two best friends in the world," said Robin.

Her hair had gotten so long this year, that's what Edie was thinking while watching her daughter, hunched over, bawling. *What a pretty girl she's turned out to be.* She reached out to touch her daughter, and Robin, at last, accepted her mother's embrace.

That was two days ago, and now he was dead, and Robin had never gotten to say good-bye, but what would she have been saying good-bye to anyway? Edie remembered sitting at her father's bedside before he died and wishing she hadn't been there because he wasn't as she wanted to remember him. His skin went from gray to blue to white, as if something were passing through him and then out again, like a small wave at low tide teasing a shoreline. Mourning was an awful feeling, a relinquishment of the soul. She would rather do anything but mourn.

Her daughter finished her cookies, got up from where she was sitting to take some more, and Edie stopped her and said, "Just take the whole thing. I've got more." Robin gave her a dark look but took the entire package and returned to her seat.

"They were the only friends I had, Mom. Do you know that I don't have any other friends?"

No, Edie didn't know that.

"I have no one now." Robin started to weep. She wept and ate.

"Hey, there are a lot of nice kids who live around here," said Edie, not knowing if it were true or not.

"They're all huge assholes," said Robin. "They don't like any of the bands I like and all they care about is what kind of jeans they're wearing, which I can't even fit into anyway. And they're completely mean to me. They used to pick on me all the time until I met Aaron and Ethan." She hiccuped. "And now they're g-o-o-o-ne," she wailed.

Edie noticed that Robin had only one row of cookies left to consume and wished she had three to five of them sitting on the table in front of her.

"I mean, don't you get sick of it?" said Robin.

"Sick of what?"

"Sick of this," said Robin, and she waved her hands in front of her body.

Edie stared at her blankly.

"Being fat? Come on, Mom. You and me. We're fat."

"I don't like that word," whispered Edie.

"You should hear what the kids say to me at school," said Robin, suddenly motivated by something other than sadness, something new and cruel, a taste that was better than all the processed sugar in the world: bitterness. "They'd say it to you, too, but like ten times worse." She put another cookie into her mouth, barely chewed it, and then it was gone. "Because you're fatter than I am. So there's more to say about you."

"I'm sorry I disappoint you," said Edie, crushed and crumpled, letting herself feel that way, letting herself sink down low.

"You don't disappoint me," said Robin. "You disappoint yourself." And then she opened her mouth as if she were about to say something even worse, as if she were about to roar, but all that came out was a pile of dark, chocolate vomit, which landed in a thick puddle on the kitchen table. Robin stared at it, and then vomited again, and Edie began to gag, too, but somehow restrained herself from letting loose entirely, from freeing whatever was trapped inside her gut.

After that day, Robin grew thin quickly. She went to the boy's funeral a week later, and the next morning she got up early and went for a jog around the block. A few weeks more, and she joined the track team. It seemed like it was only a matter of months before she looked just like all the other children in the neighborhood, while Edie remained exactly the same, alone at the kitchen table, surrounded by all her worldly pleasures.

The Golden Unicorn

LET ME TELL you a story about your father, said Edie to her daughter, Robin, who did not want to hear the story, but could not figure out how to say no.

They were in the house where Robin had grown up and hated returning, where Edie still lived, all by herself, newly abandoned by her husband with, as far as Robin could tell, nowhere else to go. Was her mother's life now spent at this kitchen table, alternating between eating and grinding all the joy out of her memories?

As a child, Robin had loved her mother's stories. Edie was an eavesdropper and a gossip, but she was also the kind of person to whom even strangers would tell their secrets. She seemed wise. She seemed warm. If she didn't know how to help, she would at least know how to make you feel better. It was only when you really got to know her that she could be kind of terrifying.

And then something shifted in Robin's adolescence, and the stories stopped. There was that one thing that happened with those two boys, of which they did not speak as a family anymore but about which Robin had been thinking for so long that it had become seamless with her self.

They were her first real boy friends, Aaron and Ethan, and they had all been in love, Aaron in love with Ethan, Robin in love with Ethan, Ethan in love with his record collection and with pills and with the two of them loving him. They had all felt so deeply for one another; for months they had sat huddled in Ethan's bedroom listening to records, actual vinyl, vinyl being better and more important than CDs for many reasons, all of which Ethan enumerated excitedly in his recently deepened voice. Yes, yes, said Aaron and Robin, fascinated with his passion, his knowledge of actual pieces of information unrelated to what they learned in high school. Once they had made out in the backseat of Aaron's car, parked in a dimly lit cul-de-sac a block away from Robin's house, the three of them taking turns kissing and touching each other, plump Robin with her gigantic breasts (the boys seemed astonished when they were finally released from her bra), little Aaron with his shaved head and squat torso, Ethan's hand squished between Robin's legs, Aaron jerking off Ethan, all of them moaning, all of them the most satisfied they had ever been in their young lives—none of them would ever feel that satisfied again—until there was nothing to do but stop, zipper, buckle, awkwardly replace breasts into bra, and then, only then, feel slightly embarrassed by their audible expressions of joy. Cigarettes lit, pills popped. Robin wrote love letters to them both a week later. Mailed them, and if they got them and read them, no one said a word. Only a few days later, Ethan was dead. It had nothing to do with them. It was his family. Issues beyond anyone's control. Aaron got too sad and was sent away. Now he lived in Seattle, and every year, around the anniversary of Ethan's death—still, after all this time!—he sent her a mix CD of their favorite bands they used to listen to when they were growing up. He ran out of favorite songs a long time ago, and now they were just on repeat. She wished she could tell him to stop sending them to her, but she didn't know how to not feel that pain. She was waiting for a new, worse pain in her life to take its place.

But after that terrible time with the boys when she was fifteen, Robin had shut down to her mother. Had it been that long? Robin was thirty-one years old. Had she really been so far away from everyone even though she was just a forty-five-minute drive into Chicago? She never said anything of substance about her life, maybe a story here and there about her work as a history teacher at a high-priced private school. The kids made her laugh. Her mother had to drag out the tiniest detail. Edie never knew when she was going to get a new piece of information, and when she did, she savored it for weeks, fleshing out her daughter's life in her head.

But what reason would Robin have to trust her

with her heart? Even if Edie was sharing her own heart with her now. No, not sharing. That was too casual a word. She was digging her fingertips into her breastbone and clawing her way inside through her skin, excavating through blood and bones, mining her flesh for that precious beating object, and then laying it in front of her daughter for her judgment. And with each story she told, each howling, moaning tale, it was as if she were striking her own heart again and again with a closed fist. Either she was resuscitating it or she was destroying it. Either she was going to live or die. Robin did not know yet which it would be.

Let me tell you a story about your father, she said.

Out back, through the screen door, an empty bird feeder, old, forgotten, spotted with mold, swung from a white oak tree in the spring wind.

But Robin had heard enough of her stories over the past two months.

She had heard about how Edie had married too young, married the first man who came along who asked, and how on their wedding night, after they'd already exchanged the "I do's" and smashed the glass and danced the hora and shoved cake into each other's face ("He really got in there," mused Edie. "I had frosting in my ears."), after they had posed for pictures with their arms around each other and danced a slow box step to "When a Man Loves a Woman" and had kissed

148

good night Edie's friends from law school and Richard's friends from pharmacy school and cousins and aunts and a few high-school friends and neighbors and Edie's parents and Richard's parents, every last one of them drunk, after all that sealing-of-the-deal, he had whispered to her in the honeymoon suite of the Drake Hotel in downtown Chicago, "Are you sure about this?" Which of course made her unsure. Great start to a life together, Richard. Nice work.

And today there was more: that terrible trip to Rome, which was supposed to be a fresh start for the two of them after the kids were out of the house, and then he ended up complaining the whole time, from the cab to O'Hare to the Vatican and back again.

"Why did he bring the wrong shoes? Did I have to do everything for him?" said Edie.

"Why didn't you just buy new shoes? You were in Italy. That's where they make the best shoes in the world," said Robin.

"Well, eventually we did, but that's not the point."

Robin put her left cheek down on the kitchen table and let out a sigh. The light had turned outside, and dusty yellow dusk approached. Dinnertime.

"Can we just eat?" said Robin. "Let's go get some food."

"What kind of food?" said Edie.

"Wherever you go to eat, Mom. I don't care."

Edie's hands, puffed up, ghostly white, twitched on the table. Robin could tell she did not want to eat in front of her. She would rather reveal the inconsistencies of her husband's lovemaking abilities. She would rather discuss his merely adequate financial planning over the last three decades. Wouldn't Robin rather hear about how her father had always loved his own mother more than his wife?

"Why don't you want to eat with me, Mom?" said Robin.

"Fine, you want to eat? Let's eat."

"I'll drive," said Robin, who'd had one glass of wine.

"I can drive," said her mother, who'd had three.

"I can't believe I'm having this discussion with you," said Robin, and while she was probably talking about how weird it was to argue with her mother, who, up until the last three months of her life, had been the kind of woman who put ice cubes in her wine, about whether or not she was sober enough to drive, she was also talking big picture here, about the life they were having together, mother and daughter swapping authority, her mother ripping open her insides and tossing whatever she felt at her daughter to see what stuck. This new life that was not much fun at all.

Robin won—"Okay, you win." "What do I win?"—and drove the two of them one town over, and then another, past the highway that went to Woodfield Mall and then farther, to Chicago, until her mother directed her into a tiny, tidy strip mall that housed a windowless sports bar, a 7-Eleven, and a cell-phone store. Robin parked in front of a Chinese restaurant—the Golden Unicorn—which was lit so brightly that the sidewalk outside the front window was a sunny yellow, and some of the light caught on her mother as they walked in through the front door, and Robin saw she was smiling, a genuine, giddy smile.

It was early, not even 5:00 P.M., and the restaurant was empty, except for a young Chinese woman sitting before a giant pile of green beans spread on a table. She stood when the two women entered and rushed toward Edie with open arms, and they quickly embraced.

"We haven't seen you in so long," she said. "We missed you."

"I haven't been feeling well," said Edie.

Was that true? Robin didn't even know if Edie felt worse one day to the next.

"Oh no," said the girl, young, slim, punkish, with a purple streak in the front of her hair, and thick black, high-laced boots over the bottoms of her tight black jeans. "We can't have you getting sick. I'll get you some tea. You sit down, and I'll get you some right away."

Robin stood there lamely, watching the two

women engaging so brightly with each other, her mother with this stranger.

Edie finally introduced Robin to the woman— Anna was her name—who broke into a broad smile and then shook Robin's hand with gusto, her slender palm disappearing into Robin's hand. "The schoolteacher! What an honor to have you here. Your mother talks about you all the time. We love your mother. Just love her. She's our hero."

Robin was stunned, and a little stung, too, that she had no idea what was going on at that moment. *Why is my mother the hero of a Chinese restaurant?*

Anna pointed to a table near the window. "Go on, sit, and I'll get you some tea and let Dad know you're here."

They sat together at the table, her mother shifting herself in uncomfortably. Fresh pink tea roses floating in a small glass jar on the table. Robin picked up the menu, but Edie told her to put it down. "Just let them take care of it," she said. "They'll bring whatever's good tonight."

Robin looked around, at the framed black-and-white photographs of faraway cities that hung on the walls, the raw wood tabletops; it felt like a place she would go to in the city, and definitely not like a restaurant next door to a place called the Billy Goat Tavern.

"It's kind of cool in here," said Robin.

"It's all Anna," said her mother. "If her father

had his way, it would look like every other Chinese restaurant in town. But Anna thinks she can get the yuppies in here."

"Is it working?" said Robin.

"It's not *not* working," said her mother. "We'll see."

Not so long before, her mother had worked for the companies that opened these strip malls all over the suburbs. She knew the businesses well, had seen them come and go. Robin's father, too, with his one pharmacy left after having three through the eighties and nineties, had his opinions on what made a business work. Robin would put her money on her mother's opinion over her father's any day of the week.

"He needs to advertise more. Spend a little more time on the Internet," Edie said. "I've been helping them out. I did some paperwork for them. It was no big deal. I have too much time on my hands anyway."

Suddenly Robin felt relief: Her mother had a life outside her home, outside of sitting there at that kitchen table, stewing in her own flesh, in the layers of hate and frustration and anger and heartbreak that she had been building up for so long. If she came here regularly, and she was helping people, then maybe she could be saved after all. Edie had always lived to help people, volunteering with the elderly, the synagogue, feeding the homeless every Christmas without fail. All those female political candidates she canvassed for. All those family members who needed pro bono work, and she did it without thinking, staying up late after Robin and her brother had gone to bed. God, where *was* that passionate, connected, committed woman? Robin missed her so. Was she right here? Sitting right in front of her? Was she still there under all that weight? Robin allowed herself to plant that tiny seed of hope within herself; she watered it with green tea, the bright lights of the Chinese restaurant sunning it.

A Chinese man in a chef's jacket sidled out of the kitchen, long lines on his face, in his forehead, on his cheeks, arched eyebrows, a tender little mustache on his upper lip; wiping his hands on a towel he then tucked neatly under his arm.

"Edith," he said.

Sure, thought Robin. It's Edith on her driver's license and her birth certificate and her voter's registration card and then *absolutely nowhere else in the world,* so why not in this Chinese restaurant?

He stood before the table and then waited calmly until Edie invited him to join them, and then he slid in next to her, patted her hand just once, and crossed his on the table in front of him.

Robin wondered if her mother knew that this man was in love with her.

"You are the famous Robin," he said.

"Yes," she said. "I am extremely famous."

"I'm Kenneth Song," he said. He studied her briefly, his eyes focusing into recognition, and then he broke into a small smile. "You look just like your mother," he said.

It took a lot from Robin to keep her mouth shut right then, because she wanted to wrinkle her forehead and purse her lips and jerk her head back in disdain, the "Are you high?" look she'd been working on since she was in her teens, popular with no one but effective nonetheless. She wanted to say to him, *How on earth do I look like a 350-pound woman?*

But maybe he knew something she didn't. Their eyes were still the same, after all, dark, intense bullets—you can't hide the eyes—and their hair the same color and texture, black kinks down to their shoulders, and maybe they had the same smile. When they smiled.

Maybe he could see right through Edie, to what was underneath.

"Same eyes," said Robin faintly.

"I have to go," he said. "Big party coming in at seven."

"That's great!" said Edie.

He slid himself out of the booth, and, before he walked away, turned gracefully to Robin and said, "Your mother is a saint."

Edie Middlestein, patron saint of Chinese joints everywhere. *Well,* thought Robin, *if my mother lives in this alternate universe in this strip mall, at least it's nice that they think she's so amazing.*

"He's got quite a story," said Edie, and she nodded approvingly at the value of such a thing. A story!

Anna came out of the kitchen and squinted up at the ceiling. "Too bright," she said, and wandered off. A moment later the lights dimmed, the final piece of the atmosphere in place, and Robin felt herself ease slightly into her seat. The restaurant was adorable. She couldn't believe that her mother had never brought her here before. She imagined briefly her whole family—minus her father, of course—dining here together, Benny and his wife and the kids. This would make her weekly trip to the suburbs more than tolerable. If there were a place they could all call their own together, in this unfortunate new phase of their lives.

But then came the food. Platter after platter of sizzling, decadent, rich, sodium-sugar-drenched food. Steaming, plush pork buns, and bright green broccoli in thick lobster sauce, sticky brown noodles paired with sweet shrimp and glazed chicken, briny, chewy clams swimming in a subtle black-bean gravy. Cilantro-infused scallion pancakes. A dozen dumplings stuffed with a curiously, addictively spicy seafood, the origin of which Robin could not determine, but it seemed irrelevant anyway.

Robin tried one bite of everything, and that was it. The patron saint of former fat girls. It was delicious, Robin would not deny Mr. Song his gift. But there was just so much food, *too much food,* and all of it was terrible for her mother. Couldn't they see who her mother was? Didn't they know that every bite her mother took was bringing her one step closer to death?

Edie seemed to be ignoring the fact that her daughter was across the table from her, or at least she did an excellent job of pretending she was alone. She ate everything on every plate, each bite accompanied with a thick forkful of white rice. Edie came and she conquered, laying waste to every morsel. Robin wondered what her mother felt like when she was done. Was it triumph? Eleven seafood dumplings, six scallion pancakes, five pork buns, the pounds of noodles and shrimp and clams and broccoli and chicken. Not that anyone was counting. Was there any guilt? Or did she hope to simply pass out and forget what had just happened?

You're killing her, Robin wanted to say. But of course it was not their fault. Because her mother was killing herself.

Later, in the car, in the parking lot, outside the sports bar, where two women in their twenties leaned against a wall sharing one cigarette, outside the 7-Eleven, where a UPS man purchased a two-liter of Coca-Cola and two overcooked hot dogs drenched in cheese sauce, outside a cell-phone store, where a bored salesgirl working her way through community college slumped behind a counter texting a girl who had pissed her off at a party the night before, outside a Chinese restaurant where the food was made with love by a man who was once an unstoppable chef, in love with his work, in love with his life, until he lost his wife to cancer and he became sad for a long time, until his daughter said, "Stop it," and now here he was, cooking again, outside of all this Edie and Robin sat, Edie staring out the window, Robin with her head against the steering wheel.

"Just drive," said Edie. "You're embarrassing me in front of them."

"You can't do this anymore," said Robin. "You can't eat like this."

"You're the one who wanted to eat," she said, and she started to cry quietly and to herself.

"I don't want you to die," said Robin.

"I didn't know you cared," said Edie.

"Stop it," said Robin. "Don't pull that on me. Don't try to make me feel bad for being me."

They didn't say anything for a while, watching everything shift in the strip mall, the two girls crushing their smokes under their heels then sharing a stick of gum, the UPS driver exiting the lot, one hot dog already half eaten before he pulled out onto the road, the girl in the cell-phone store showing a text to a co-worker, cursing loudly, sending a customer scuttling out the front door. They watched a party of seven, a birthday party, walk into the restaurant. They were good tippers, even if you couldn't tell it by looking at them.

"I'm here now, aren't I?" said Robin, but neither one of them knew if it was already too late.

Male Pattern

BENNY MIDDLESTEIN WOKE up one day and realized he was going bald, and he thought: *"This is the end, beautiful friend."* He'd always had a perfectly thick head of hair—he had even come out of the womb with his rosy pink head covered in dark fuzz—and there had been no indication that he would ever have had anything to worry about for the rest of his life, at least when it came to his hair. Other things, they were maybe more of a problem.

His daughter's newfound adolescent moodiness, those dark, twisted, frustrated glances she shot him whenever he opened his mouth, as if an *Oh, my God, Dad* were just hovering in the air between them, waiting to be splattered up against him, a condescending pie in the face. He remembered when his little sister had gone sour in her teens. Once the milk turned, there was no turning it back. Yes, his daughter was something to worry about.

There was also his wife's full-blown obsession with his mother's weight and her diabetes, it was all she talked about, first thing in the morning, staring straight up at the ceiling in bed. Not that it didn't need talking about, so he couldn't argue with her necessarily, only sometimes maybe, just for a day, he wished they could take a break.

But there she was, squirreled up next to him under the comforter, frowning, making all kinds of new lines in her forehead.

"I'm worried," she said.

"I know you're worried," he said. *If you keep making that face, it'll stay that way,* is what he wanted to say.

"Aren't you worried? Why aren't you worried more?"

"I'm worried plenty."

He put a pillow over his face and inhaled the fabric softener, chemical approximation of a mountain breeze.

At night, too, she was fixated on *this life and death situation,* after the kids went to bed, during what was supposed to be their quiet time together, out back, sharing a joint.

"Can't you just relax?" he said. He rubbed her shoulders, narrow, fragile, wrenched up with worry. "Take another hit."

"This stuff will kill you," she said.

"We've been smoking this for twenty years," he said.

"I've been meaning to talk to you about that," she said.

She was not wearing her mortality well, a real shame for such a pretty girl.

And there were e-mails during the day.

Sometimes there were texts, and she hated texting, the squinting and the poking. But Rachelle had been following his mother around like some undercover cop, tracking her eating, and it was not enough that she contain this knowledge within herself.

She's at the Superdawg on Milwaukee. 3 hot dogs!!!

He had tried to tell his wife to stop following her, but even saying the words made him feel like he was falling from the sky, a loose and lurching sensation in his gut. He searched for the right thing to say, because it all just seemed so preposterous, that they were even having this conversation. *You're freaking me out,* was he allowed to say that? *Please don't stalk my mother anymore.*

"I know you're just trying to help," he said. "But I'm not sure how she would feel about it." This was over lunch, a small, sunny diner near the synagogue, where they had just dropped off the kids for their haftorah lesson with the cantor. They were both eating salads covered in raw vegetables; that was all they ever ate lately. Rachelle had ordered for them both without asking him what he wanted. Oil and vinegar on the side.

He salted and peppered his salad when she went to the bathroom.

"I think she has a right to privacy," he said, head bowed, one fleck of red, raw onion trapped on a back molar, stubbornly resisting his tongue's ministrations.

"That's like saying someone who is about to jump off the roof of a building should be allowed to enjoy the view first," she said. She pushed the salad away from her, half eaten, and gave it a disgusted glance. "I specifically told her no croutons," she said. "You heard me, right?"

"I heard you," he said, cowed, covering his mouth with his hand and reaching one finger quickly inside to free the onion from his tooth.

"Just give her a break," he said.

"You won't be telling me to give her a break when she's dead," said Rachelle, and he suddenly missed that fleck of onion, a simple problem he could solve with a small gesture.

He was worried about his mother, even if Rachelle didn't believe it. He was worried about his mother, two surgeries down, maybe another on the way, and he was worried about his daughter and his wife, who had both forgotten how to smile, and he was, on a smaller scale, worried about his father, who seemed adrift and sad now that he had left Benny's mother and was playing the field, the sixty-year-old suburbanite field, which he couldn't imagine was a particularly fun field, and, for the first time in his life, he was least worried about his sister, who, he was pretty sure, even as closed off as she was, as unrelentingly cranky, might actually have met someone and fallen in love.

But his hair! He'd always had his hair, his crown of glory: thick, jet-black, with jaunty waves that set it slightly on its end. He wore it a half inch longer than his conservative co-workers did, and he liked to believe that it gave him a youthful edge over them. In college, he'd worn it even longer and had busy sideburns as well, which gave him a grubby bad-boy look, as bad as a ZBT at the University of Illinois could be. His hair was one of the things that had drawn Rachelle to him; he wasn't as boisterous as his brothers, he didn't push for the easy joke, not because he was shy— he was plenty funny, he thought—but because he was usually extremely stoned. Still, in the corner by the stereo, at an off-campus party thrown by one of the brothers, a purple-green-swirled glass bong someone had brought back from his summer travels in Amsterdam seated before him, strong, silent, fit, slightly pie-eyed, with a tight T-shirt, tight Levi's, and I-don't-give-a-shit flip-flops, and with a head of hair so thick there was no way he didn't have a kick-ass gene pool, Benny got the hottest girl in the room without lifting much more than that bong to his lips.

Forever he'd had that hair. That was the one thing he should not have had to worry about, and yet there it was, sliding off his head every morning in the shower like sunburned skin after a weekend at the beach. There was now a significant bald spot on the back of his head, and the hair at his temples had started to recede. He could only wonder what would happen next: Would his body shrink, too, into the shape of a frail old man, and would his wife eventually reject him? Was he dying? Or was he merely getting old?

Even as the answers sat right before him, that perhaps all this worry about his wife, his mother, his daughter, and on and on, had manifested itself so obviously in a physical way, he refused to believe that it was as simple (although, of course, it was not simple at all) as that, and so he went to see Dr. Harris, a good guy, a straight shooter, and also the owner of a nice head of hair himself, his graying and cut short but still thick and attractive.

"It could be a number of things," said Dr. Harris. "Genetics, that's first on the list."

"It's not genetic," said Benny, his legs swinging slightly from the exam table, 8:00 A.M. on a Monday, an urgent appointment after a weekend of hair loss. "Not on my mother's side, not on my father's side. No one's bald."

"Stress is another possibility," the doctor said gently to Benny. They belonged to the same synagogue, and their wives were in a book club together, and he had heard all about Rachelle lately, how she had insisted the last time they had all met (they were discussing *The Help*) that pastries no longer be served at their meetings. No pastries, no cheese, no crackers. Just crudités, and don't even try to sneak ranch dip in there, she wouldn't hear of it; ranch dip was *all sugar*. There was nothing wrong with making a dietary request, but it was the way that she said it. She was violent in her articulation—"I swear to God, she almost sounded British," said his wife—and she was righteous. No wine either. Empty calories. As a doctor, Roger Harris technically had to agree with Rachelle, but as a human being he wondered if she had gone off the deep end. ("What's the point of having a book club if you don't get to eat brownies and drink wine?" said his wife. "Otherwise I'll just stay home.")

Benny stared at his doctor, the wise man, the trusted source of knowledge. He wanted to be able to talk to him about his problem; he wanted to be able to talk to anyone. He used to be able to talk to his wife about everything. They had been on the same team since they were seniors in college. There was an accidental pregnancy, and there was no question they'd be getting married, keeping those babies, the twins, twice as much to love. They were in this life together. And now she was the problem, one of them anyway. He couldn't bring himself to admit out loud to this relative stranger sitting before him that the best part of his life had suddenly become the worst. Still, he was no liar.

"Who doesn't have stress?" said Benny. "I think there's something wrong with you if you don't have it. But this much?" He pointed to his head with both index fingers.

"I can do some tests," said the doctor. He rattled off a list, but Benny wasn't listening, he was thinking of his mother's health. Her diabetes was taking her down fast, and he felt so helpless; he didn't think a raw-vegetable diet was going to make a difference. Benny jerked back just as the doctor handed him a prescription for Propecia.

"In the short term, if you can, take a couple of vacation days. Get a massage. You might consider finding someone to talk to about whatever it is you're going through. There are some great therapists here in the building, and I'm pretty sure they're on your insurance plan." He leaned forward and tapped Benny on the knee with his clipboard. "Hey, there's no shame in getting a little help."

Benny looked down at the clipboard, not at the doctor. Clearly he didn't know where he came from, how his family operated. Therapy was for people who had an interest in communication. This was not the Middlestein family, at least not anymore.

"So set up an appointment with Marnie at the front desk for those tests, and we'll look at next steps from there," Dr. Harris said. They shook hands, like men, firmly, seriously, with intent.

Benny did not set up an appointment with

Marnie at the front desk. He did head to his father's pharmacy, though, prescription in hand. He would be late for work, but he did not care. All this craziness had started because his father had left his mother after she got sick, and if he were still there to take care of her and nurse her back to health, none of this would be happening.

He drove quickly, occasionally catching a glimpse of his head in the rearview mirror. He was unable to resist adjusting the mirror at a stoplight, angling it at his head; was it so thin he could see the sunlight through it now?

There was nothing wrong with him, except for his family.

In the corner of the mini-mall, across from the Polish-owned hair and nail salon, sat his father's last pharmacy, the final, fading jewel in his empire. Once there were three. Now there was just one, with cracked linoleum and an outdated greeting-card section. Walgreens was cheaper and had a far superior skin-care section.

But his father's clientele persisted. He had been the first Jewish pharmacist to set up shop in the area, and he had collected his customers from all the other lonely Jews who had moved northwest of the city and the lake in the 1970s, looking for an affordable new home and an easy commute, not thinking far ahead enough as to how they would build a community for themselves. Well, you start small, as it turns out. Richard and nine other men—how had he managed to pull a *minyan* together?—regularly meeting in the back room of the pharmacy. Praying, and then plotting for a future: regular services, first at the local high-school auditorium, so many Jews crawling out of the woodwork to attend, happy to find a place where they didn't have to explain why they put all their bread away once a year, or why there wasn't a Christmas tree in their front window, or why they drove so far just to get some decent whitefish salad. Why the phrase "Jew down" wasn't acceptable, under any circumstances. There was a cantor fresh from school, a rabbi who had left another synagogue in Ohio under veiled but ultimately innocuous circumstances and wanted to start over, investors, believers, narcissists—they all threw in, did whatever it took to build something out of nothing, a place to worship from an empty plot of unincorporated land surrounded by oak trees stretching far back to a tiny stream where deer gathered sometimes in the summer. A beautiful place to be yourself.

The synagogue members all supported Middlestein Drugs for years, enabling Richard to open one more and then another across the northwest suburbs. The eighties were a good time for everyone. But then the family business began to slowly crumble, like a sick tree limb infested with a mysterious fungus. There were a few causes: More conservative members of the synagogue branched off to create their own competing temple a few towns over. People moved out of the area, or died. And a younger membership emerged at the synagogue he helped found, and they knew nothing of Richard's past, and had no loyalties to him. All they knew was that he owned and operated these dusty pharmacies he never bothered to modernize or renovate. He had made a mistake, it seemed. He thought that being a contributing member of his community, being a Good Jew, would be enough to make his business thrive. But this was no small town; this was a *suburb*. An American suburb, no less. Keep up with the Walgreens and the Targets and the Kmarts and the Walmarts, or get out, Mr. Middlestein. Get out.

Benny pushed through the front door, an ancient bell jingling above his head, and barreled past the aisles, the snack aisle, the makeup and skin-care aisle, feminine hygiene, dental care, shampoo, vitamins, over-the-counter medications, breast pumps and crutches, enemas, an aisle and a half of them, why were there so many enemas? The place needed a good dusting. One of his father's delivery boys, a mentally challenged man named Scotty who had worked there since Benny was in college, was intensely mopping the same few squares of linoleum. He wasn't allowed to drive a car, but he had a bright blue bike with a basket, which he would ride with deliveries to the homes of all the elderly shut-ins nearly year-round, even in the cold. The only thing that would stop him was the snow, and then he would simply trudge miles each way. "It gives me something to do," Scotty had told Benny once. "Otherwise I'd just be getting into trouble." Was this his father being a positive part of the community by hiring someone who might have otherwise had trouble finding a job, or a cheap bastard? Benny could never decide.

His father, his thick gray hair almost entirely intact, was seated at a stool behind the counter, hunched over, a sturdy tree bent with the wind, poking at his cell phone with a pen. He looked up as Benny approached, and a smile rolled across his face. *Benny!* And then, squinting, he noticed his son's hair, and then his forehead folded in on itself, and his smile withered slightly.

"This is a surprise," he said. He reached his hand out across the counter to his son, and Benny grasped it faintly, which was not how he had been taught to shake hands at all. Richard was still staring at Benny's head. They hadn't seen each other in a month. One month was all it took for a man to lose half his hair. Richard reflexively reached for his own hair, as if to confirm it was still all there, and Benny winced.

"Are you sick?" said Richard. "What's going on here?"

Benny, suddenly trembling, handed Richard the prescription.

"I don't know, Dad. I don't know what's going on."

Richard motioned his head toward the door to the back room. It had never been painted, even after all these years, and a fake brass handle drooped half out of its socket. "Let's go in back and talk," he said. "Come on, kiddo."

Benny looked down, that loose, out-of-control feeling ranging around his gut again. Had he come here for advice? He was still angry with his father for leaving his mother when she was so sick, and he didn't understand how Richard had let her get that way in the first place. Rachelle had banned his father from their house months before. "He has nothing good to teach our children," is what she had said. Everything was falling apart because of this man. And yet, here he was, standing in front of him, about to spill his guts, looking for a little wisdom. Maybe, just maybe, he knew something Benny didn't.

Richard called Scotty to him—Scotty dragging his mop and bucket slowly down the aisle—and asked him to keep watch over the counter, and Scotty replied with a long and meaningful salute, as if he were a soldier in the delivery-boy army, followed by a quiet giggle to himself.

Benny followed his father into the back room, a dark, cobweb-ridden space lined with rusted-out shelving units.

"What did the doctor say?" Richard peered at

the prescription. "Dr. Harris, he's all right. You could do worse."

"Stress, probably," said Benny.

"That's a lot of stress." He motioned to Benny's hair and made a *whoosh* sound.

"Yeah, well, I am under a lot of stress, Dad, what with my parents getting divorced and my mother practically on her deathbed. How about you?" Benny was pissed. Were they going to be coy suddenly? Were they going to pretend that the last few months hadn't happened?

His father turned from him and shuffled off between the shelving units, and didn't say anything, it turned icy quiet, spiders froze in their webs, and Benny could hear Scotty singing "The Star-Spangled Banner" through the door. Finally Richard returned, red-faced, with a pill bottle in hand. Benny waited for him to explode. Benny felt a delicious anticipation take hold of him; he craved some sort of show of emotion from his grunting, withdrawn, disappointed father.

But Richard kept himself calm, handing his son the bottle, and then taking two steps back and rubbing his hands together, some imaginary dust flicking off onto the floor.

He said, "We make the decisions we make, Benny. We cannot take them back. I am not a perfect person." Benny watched as his father chose his words, plucked them from deep within his heart. "I can only tell you this: Your mother was making me crazy. Not normal crazy. Crazy crazy. Like it was going to kill me."

"How bad could it have been to spend the rest of your life with the mother of your children?" said Benny, surprised at his own calm. "She was loyal to you. And that should mean something."

"There was nothing left inside," said Richard. He took a few more steps back and leaned against the wall for support. "I was a bag of bones. There was nothing else in there. Whatever kept me standing, that was it, that was all that was left."

"You didn't put up a fight," said Benny.

"I'm trying to be respectful here, but have you not met your mother?" said Richard. "You can't fight her. You should know that by now."

That didn't sound right to Benny. Even if you can't fight, you should at least try to fight. He didn't know if he could fight his wife and win. They'd always gotten along so well; only recently had he begun to understand what kind of whirlwinds of power and aggression had lain dormant within her. He wondered briefly if he'd married someone like his mother, who, he had to admit, his father was right about; she was one tough cookie. But then he remembered that Rachelle was his petite princess, and how she was usually so calm, almost regal, most of the time, unlike his mother, who was boisterous and overflowing, and yes, Rachelle knew how to get what she wanted, just like his mother, but the similarities began and ended there.

He was relieved. It was not like he hadn't had this conversation with himself before, but every once in a while it was nice to remind yourself you had not turned into your worst nightmare, this man standing before him, who had just handed him a bottle full of pills intended to save his hair. He hadn't realized until that moment that being his father would be his worst nightmare, because his father had never been that person before, until he decided to be single and sixty and lonely, just him and Scotty hanging out in the fluorescent-lit pharmacy all day long, Scotty singing patriotic songs to Richard, the two of them waiting for the next old Jew to walk through the front door in search of Cardizem or hand cream or an enema. Benny and his father had hit the end of the line together; it was up to Benny to figure it, love, marriage, life, the universe, all of it out, by himself.

The two of them wandered uselessly out to the pharmacy; Benny would never step foot into that back room again until after his father had died a decade later, and there was no question that the business would be closed (it probably should have been closed five years before, but Richard had refused, saying that he offered a service to the community, though Benny knew that it was just because he needed a place to go all day), that the dusty shelves needed to be emptied and then tossed out the back door, a painful, clanking, depressing act that Benny, entirely bald by then, accomplished quietly, sadly, on his own.

But for now, the Propecia was on the house, and Richard walked Benny to the front door.

"So maybe I can come by sometime?" said Richard.

"I don't think so," said Benny. "Not yet. I'll work on it."

They stopped and stared at each other, and there were a million things of a confrontational nature that still hovered between them, but Benny wondered if they were worth the battle, and then decided they were not, or that his father wasn't worth it anyway, and he would deal with how sad that made him feel some other time.

Instead he said, "I always wondered something. Why do you carry so many kinds of enemas? Wouldn't just one kind do the trick?"

"You'd be surprised," said his father.

Dinner was something related to kale and beets. If he could have gotten back on the expressway and returned to his office and spent the night working, he would have. There was something so intensely satisfying about number crunching; he could almost feel the delicate little digits crumbling in his fist, piles forming and then towering on his desk, magically disappearing overnight so that each day there was the challenge to create a higher pile of numbers than the day before. He didn't see it as a pointless task; he saw it as a game he got to play every single day, and no matter what, he always won.

But he would not abandon his children to contend with this madness alone. They were in it together, Benny and the kids. Josh had surreptitiously eaten six pieces of tasteless multigrain bread slathered in soy butter. He would never complain, he would just adapt, until it was too late: the curse of the Middlestein men. Emily, dark-eyed and dangerous and glowering from the other end of the table, insistently made eye contact with her father, at one point openly staring at him while simultaneously stabbing her fork vengefully and noisily into the food on her plate. Rachelle ignored her, instead focusing on cutting her food into the tiniest of squares, which she would then chew thoughtfully and slowly, as if she were savoring every vitamin, as if she could *feel* each bite extending her life span. Rachelle, alone, finished all the food on her plate.

It must be so nice to feel so right all the time, he thought. He would ask her that later. What that felt like.

After dinner, after Benny had done the dishes (defiantly dumping the remaining purplish mess into the garbage, because *no he would not* be taking the leftovers to work the next day), after the kids watched whatever crappy reality television show they were emotionally invested in that week, after they practiced their haftorah readings for their upcoming b'nai mitzvah, their voices reverberating sweetly from the living room, and after Rachelle forced Josh to try on his new suit for his father, Josh executing a glamorous turn as if he were on a runway—that kid had moves—before suddenly turning, embarrassed, and then running back upstairs again, and after the kids went to bed early, which is something that had not occurred ever in their house, Benny and Rachelle stood out in the backyard, near the tarp-covered swimming pool, and shared a joint, Rachelle taking just one hit before proclaiming, "That is the last time I am ever smoking this stuff ever again." (This was not a lie, she meant it as fact, but it was untrue nevertheless.)

"Whatever," said Benny.

"Don't whatever me," said Rachelle.

Benny took a walk around the pool, stopping on the far side, then taking a step back and peering up at the house he had paid off nearly all on his own, only the down payment coming from Rachelle's parents, a dowry of sorts, he supposed, or at least some sort of panicked gesture toward the then-young couple who had gotten pregnant before they had even graduated from college. It was a simple mistake in the bathroom of his fraternity house, his intention being merely to hoist her up onto the sink and get her off with his tongue, but it tasted so good, too good, and then he stood and plunged inside of her without protection, their eyes locked together, it was just supposed to be for a minute, just one more minute, and then he would return to his duties downstairs, but neither of them could stop themselves, they were making nonsensical noises, they were having nonsensical thoughts, and he, deft, mathematical, precise Benny, made a serious miscalculation.

"Uh-oh," he had said.

"Uh-oh?" she had said.

And now look at this house, brick, Colonial style with two sturdy pillars in the front that made Benny feel safe, like his family would be protected, two stories, three bedrooms, two and a half baths, a sunny kitchen, a shaded living room, a wet bar in the basement, a backyard with room enough for a swimming pool, a luxurious deck, and a badminton net in the summertime. (There was talk of building a gazebo, but not until after he saw what this year's bonus was like.) A garage, with two sumptuous Lexuses in it. A shed with one of those lawn mowers you can ride. Not that he ever mowed his lawn. There was a guy who did that. He didn't know who the guy was; his wife took care of all of that kind of stuff. Rachelle took care of him, that's right, he reminded himself. He had trusted her to do so for so long. But he needed to eat. His kids needed to eat.

"We're hungry," he said to Rachelle.

"There was plenty of food on that table tonight," she said.

"The kids are still growing. They need more than just vegetables," he said. "And I'm suddenly going bald if you hadn't noticed."

"There is no scientific evidence linking hair loss to eating more vegetables," she said.

He threw his hands up in the air, gestured toward the sky, and then toward his head, and then back again.

"It's true," she said. "I looked it up on the Internet."

He took another hit from his joint and then realized he was high, and hungrier than ever, and there was not a goddamn thing in the house worth eating. He wondered if she would notice if he went for a walk and hit up the closest fast-food place, a McDonald's about a half mile away. Maybe he would sneak back some fries for the kids. She'd probably smell it on him, though. He'd never make it past the first floor.

And then a scream rang out in the cool spring air, and Benny tossed his joint without thinking (this would eventually be found by the guy who mowed the lawn, in this case an Illinois State student on summer vacation, who would pocket it in one slippery motion and then later smoke it blissfully in his pickup truck during his lunch break) and ran toward the front of the house, two steps behind Rachelle, the scream sending shivers up his arms and the back of his neck. It was a child's scream, he was certain. *Don't stop for nothing, Middlestein.* He rounded the corner and saw Emily, lying on the ground, her head cracked open, her arm pointed in a strange direction, as if it were trying to flee her body. Benny glanced up at the house: Her second-floor window was open, and Josh peered out of it, his mouth shaped like an O. Then Rachelle was by her side, and so was he; both of them were bent over her, both of them terrified as they had never been before, their fear only receding after the stitches, after the twenty-four-hour watch-for-a-concussion period was over, and after the cast was put on. ("It was a clean break," the doctor assured them, and they repeated this phrase over and over to anyone who would listen, as if focusing on this one positive thing would spin the entire incident into the plus category.) And when their heart rates returned to normal, and Rachelle stopped with her crying jags, and Emily was no longer in the worst pain of her life, and her grandparents had come and gone (separately, of course) with books and balloons and chocolates, and Benny finally said to his daughter, "What were you doing?" and Emily replied, "I just had to get out of there," Benny did not even turn and look at his wife to see her expression, because he already knew what she was thinking, what she *had* to be thinking or she was not the woman he had married and she had been fooling him all this time, which was, "Enough is enough already."

Edie, 332 Pounds

AS PART OF her early-retirement package, the law firm where she had worked for thirty-three years had extended her the opportunity to keep her health care at an extremely low rate until death or something better came along. She also received her pension plan in full, and on top of that, a not-unfair amount of money to keep her mouth shut about the fact that they were letting her go mainly because her weight distressed the three new partner-owners of the firm, who were all children of the people who had originally hired Edie straight out of law school, freshly married, not yet pregnant, a much slimmer version of herself. She had, at various times in her life, been a more righteous person, more prone to moral outrage, a scrapper, and that person would have considered this not nearly enough money in exchange for being discriminated against, that there was not enough money in the world to allow someone to say to you—without actually *saying* it, mind you—*You're fat, now will you please go away?*

But Edie was exhausted, the whole world tired her, and in a humiliated moment she accepted their offer, even smiled while she shook their hands. Maybe this was a chance to reboot. She wanted more time to spend with her grand-children. A month later her doctor told Edie her diabetes had worsened, and that he would have to have a stent inserted into her leg, to make that awful, cramping pain she (mostly) refused to admit she was in go away. She might even need a bypass someday. She could get sicker, he told her. She could die. Then she was suddenly grateful for the health care and the money in the bank, and also the time to recover from all her wounds.

The first surgery was tomorrow morning. Down the hall her son, Benny, slept in his old bedroom; he would be driving her to Evanston at 6:00 A.M., so that her husband could go to the pharmacy he owned later in the morning and sign for some deliveries, which apparently no one else on the entire planet could sign for except him. She wouldn't even think of asking her daughter, Robin, who lived downtown, to spend the night in her home. It was hard enough to get her to come to dinner.

She lay awake now, her brain, like always, running a million miles a minute even if she herself moved so slowly it sometimes was like she was not even in motion at all. She was thinking about food, specifically a value-size package of kettle-baked sea salt potato chips and a plastic tub of deli onion dip she had purchased from the Jewel that afternoon, which were sitting down-stairs in her kitchen, waiting for her like two friends who had come over for coffee and a little chitchat.

But it was after midnight, and she had been instructed not to eat anything eight to twelve hours before her surgery, and she was scheduled to have her leg cut into at 8:00 A.M. So here she was, on the tail end of acceptable timing, wondering how much damage she would really do to herself if she had a few potato chips, we're talking just a handful, and some of that cool, salty dip, and that dip was not even *like* solid food, it was like drinking a glass of milk, and those potato chips were so airy, one bite and they were over. Poof. What she was thinking about eating wouldn't even fill up one of her pinkies. All she had to do was get up out of bed, and go downstairs, and then she would be reunited with her two new best friends.

Her husband snored next to her seemingly innocently, uselessly. The most he had done for her lately was bring home her prescriptions, but he was a pharmacist! He had been bringing home her prescriptions their entire life together. Sorry, Middlestein. No points. He did not turn in his sleep; he picked a position and stuck with it all night. Not one tussle with the universe for that one, she thought.

What she didn't know was that he had been plotting all day the right way and time to leave her, and that in six more months, a few weeks before she had a second surgery, on a Friday afternoon, he would announce that he did not love her anymore and that he had not for a long time and he believed she felt the same, and for both of their sakes, for both of their lives, he was going to take the step of walking out that door and never coming back. There was also the not-so-subtle subtext of his wanting to have sex again with somebody in this lifetime, though obviously not with Edie herself. He had left so quickly, like the goddamn *coward* he was—he had taken nothing with him except for his clothes, which, while she was at Costco, he had packed in the luggage they got for that terrible trip to Italy—that she hadn't had a chance to argue with him, and what would she have said? He was probably right.

Still, she will be sad when the split finally happens. She will weep to her son and daughter, although at least a small portion of those outbursts will be calculated to make them hate their father. After a while she will stop being sad that he's gone because she'll realize she doesn't miss him, and then she will be sad because she's spent so long with someone she doesn't even miss, and then after that she'll be more sad because she realizes she *does* miss him, or at least having someone around, even if they didn't speak to each other that much. In the end, it had just been nice to know that someone was in the room, she will tell Benny, even though that is kind of a fucked-up thing to say to a son about his father. (But Edie was never one for self-control.) And now the room was empty. Just her. Just Edie. She knew that there were even more things to be sad about, so many layers of sadness yet to be unfolded. She had lived an entire life already, and now here was another one she had to start living fresh from the beginning.

Right now, though, the night before her first surgery, her only consideration was the potato chips and the onion dip, party food, a mere appetizer, but this was no party. Tomorrow a tiny metal tube would be inserted into her leg. It was not a big deal as far as surgeries went, although no one was happy with the idea of her being cut open in the first place. But she would be able to walk the same as always, even the same day. There would be some pain and some painkillers. She was going to be okay, though. She came from sturdy Russian stock, she kept telling herself, even though her father had died before he turned sixty. If only he hadn't smoked, if only he hadn't drank. If only she didn't eat.

She rose from her bed, and traveled along the same floorboards she had been traveling on for thirty-five years, the only ones that didn't creak beneath her, the only ones that would not wake her husband. She had worn a slight path in the carpeting above the floor, but they had never bothered to replace it. It was a room they spent little time in, lights out, good night, that's it. The carpeting was blue and nubby and stained with who-knows-what. The diamond-checked wallpaper curling at the ends. The curtains hadn't been opened in decades. The room was sealed from the outside world.

With her eyes shut, she could walk the path from her bed, down the hallway past Benny's and Robin's old bedrooms, their high-school graduation photos hanging on the wall outside each, their bathroom that had become hers, a place for her to hide her naked self, down the stairs, all of which creaked, but by then she was home free in her own home—Richard would never hear a thing; then through the living room, where the carpeting was newer though not new, a sky-gray plush frieze purchased when the grandchildren were younger, somewhere soft for them to play, and it had always felt nice under her feet when she made this nightly journey to the kitchen, the last stop before the linoleum, washed-out orange daisies on scuffed yellow-and-brown tile. Thirty-five years ago that tile had cheered her up every morning, and now, like everything else, it was just another surface to cross until she reached the food she desired.

She pushed through the swinging doorway to the kitchen and choked out a cry: There sat Benny, a book in front of him, a cup of coffee, a chocolate chip cookie on a plate, a stale, pained look on his face. He had been waiting awhile for her. He could not rest until she did.

"What's up, Mom?" he said. "You thirsty?"

"I was . . . yes, thirsty." Dazed, she went to a cabinet and pulled out a glass, walked to the refrigerator and pressed the glass up into the built-in ice dispenser, then leaned against the refrigerator. "Should I go back to bed?"

"It's your house, you can do whatever you want," he said. He closed the book in front of him. It was a Harry Potter book. He pointed to it, a little embarrassed. "The kids like them, I wanted to see what it was all about."

"Any good?" she said. She poured some water into the glass from a Brita on the counter, and then sat down at the table with him.

Benny, not as tall as his father, but better looking, smoother skin, tamer eyebrows, a warmer heart, *he had turned out so well,* considered the book with a back-and-forth of his head. "Goes quick," he said. "They like things that move fast, those two."

"They're both so bright," said Edie. "And good-looking. And funny."

"All right, all right, Grandma, we know you're crazy about them. Don't go giving them a big head." He had been a jokey, sweet kid, and he had grown into a jokey, sweet man.

She took a big gulp of her water, and restrained herself from pushing her lie too far and letting out a satisfied *Ahhh.* She tapped her fingers on the table, her paltry wedding ring barely giving off a shimmer. "So why are you up? Are you having trouble sleeping?"

"One hundred percent I don't want to be sitting down here," he said. "But the doctor told me that it was important for a number of reasons you have an empty stomach before the surgery." *Your weight,* he didn't say. *Your heart,* he didn't say. *Your health, your life, your death.* "I just wanted to remind you about that. In case you had forgotten."

"I'm just getting some water," she said.

"And I'm just reading a book," he said.

Six months later, he sat in the kitchen the night before another surgery. And again she rose from her bed in hopes he would not be there, and again he stopped her from eating. It was something good he could do for this person even though it was hard because it made him feel powerful in a way he never wanted. He respected his mother, because she had raised him with love, and because she was a smart woman, even though she was also so incredibly stupid. Also, he respected humanity in general. He respected a person's right to weakness. For all these reasons, he never told anyone he stayed up late waiting for his mother, not even his wife. What happened in that kitchen was between Benny and Edie. With grace he offered her his love and protection, and she accepted it, tepidly, warily. It did not bring them closer together, but it did not tear them apart.

The Walking Wounded

EMILY AND HER grandmother, Edie, walked around the track of the high school she would attend the next fall so slowly, so grudgingly, that it was possible it did not even count as exercise at all. Could one walk with loathing? They were doing it.

Emily, sharp-eyed, a ripe plum of a girl, with golden brown hair like her mother, was still tender from falling from the second story of her house one week before, her arm in a cast, a few stitches on her temple. Her grandmother, obese, sweating, limping, had had two surgeries in the past year. There could be another one at any minute, that's what Emily's parents were saying. A bigger one, way worse than the other two. A bypass.

"Look at you two, the walking wounded," her father had joked an hour earlier, leaning delicately on his Lexus, watching them shuffle off in the direction of the high school.

"Pah," her grandmother had said, and slung her hand behind her dismissively, not even bothering to look at him.

"Exactly," Emily had said. "What she said."

"I can't help it if you two are adorable," he

yelled. "Grandmother and granddaughter. Two generations!"

"What a sap," said Edie.

They *barely* made it to the track, and now they were *barely* making it around the track, the required mile, required by Emily's mother, who had lately been determined to save Edie's life.

"Have you noticed your father is going bald?" said Edie.

"It's weird, right?" said Emily.

It had happened suddenly, her father's hair loss; one day he was good-looking, with a full head of hair, younger than all the other dads at his school, sprightly and in love with her mother, and Emily had felt safe in her own home and in the world around her.

And then all these things happened at once: Her grandmother was diagnosed with diabetes and a whole bunch of other little things that went along with it, then her grandfather left her grandmother so that he could date weird women he met on the Internet (she had heard her father tell her mother), and her mother freaked the eff out. Holy crap, she had never seen her so crazy in her entire life, and her mom was already definitely an obsessive type, her hair, the house, the furniture, the carpeting, the lawn, Emily's hair, Josh's hair, their grades, their b'nai mitzvah, everyone else's hair, and on and on, everything had to be perfect. She swore if her mother could adjust the color of the sky to match her own eyes, she would, just so it could be just right.

In the middle of all this, Emily found herself surprisingly full of this really intense but deeply satisfying hate. She was a *hater* all of a sudden. She had negative things to say about her twin brother Josh (dopey, a pushover, sometimes even wimpy), her girlfriends at school (talked about boys so much, *too* much, weren't there other things to talk about? Like music or television or movies or books or crazy grandparents, anything but boys), and her homework (a waste of time, boring, repetitive, and fifty other words that all equaled one big snooze).

And don't even get her started on her mother, the intensity of Emily's emotions in opposition to her mother's very *being* were so strong that it had propelled her, late at night, out her window one week before, across the roof, and over to the tall, Colonial-style pillars that guarded the front porch, which she attempted to cling to and slide down, immediately flopping out onto the front driveway, slamming her head on the ground, and breaking her left arm neatly, in fact, so neatly that it inspired her doctor to say, "You got lucky," which made her laugh, and also her parents, too, because of course no one in that room felt lucky.

It was not even that surprising when her father started to go bald, entire chunks of hair disappearing every day, as if an evil hair troll snuck into his bedroom every night while he slept and whisked it off his head and into the night. Here was another thing that was happening to someone she knew and loved. Here was another thing that was wrong with the world. Add it to the list of Things That Suck, an actual, brand-new list that existed in a journal that she kept in her locker at school, seemingly the only place safe in the universe from her mother or the cleaning woman, Galenka, who had been tending to their house for so long that she felt perfectly entitled to invade every part of Emily's room, which was fine when she'd been five, but not when she was nearly thirteen.

"Mortality"—that was a word she had learned recently, something that had been discussed in Hebrew school. She had heard it before, she knew what it meant, but it had never applied before. Life in the biblical world was so fragile. Everyone was afraid of death at any moment. Everything was so epic, there was so much potential for disaster, storms, floods, pestilence. Diabetes (now also on the Things That Suck list) felt biblical. So did baldness. Never before had Emily realized that the world was so heavy, as heavy as her grandmother's flesh heaving next to her on the high-school track, so heavy that she could feel it balancing on her neck and back. She believed that her brother did not feel the same weight as her. She pitied him for his blindness, and she envied him for his freedom, and if she had known just a few months before, during more innocent times, that she would feel that way for the rest of her life, not just about Josh but about a lot of people in the world, which is to say (in a polite way) *conflicted,* she would have treasured those unaware, nonjudgmental, preadolescent moments more thoroughly. (Oh, to be eleven again!) Because once you know, once you really know how the world works, you can't unknow it.

And now Emily was starting to know.

"No one in our family is bald," huffed her grandmother. "The whole thing is ridiculous. We come from strong stock."

On the far side of the high school's parking lot, there was a baseball field; a visiting team warmed up, a coach cracking pop-ups to the outfield. Even from a distance, the baseball players looked tall to her. The idea of being older and bigger made her tingle. She could not wait to get to high school. She was absolutely certain that things would be better in high school: the classes, the people, the quality of life.

"I don't think people even understand how strong our gene pool is," said her grandmother. "You've got a lot of Russian blood in you. Russians are built to withstand winter."

Emily could admit that her life wasn't so bad now, and that getting older and bigger meant that there were more risks involved. She just wanted more out of it. Couldn't she do better? Couldn't everyone just do a little bit better?

"Your great-grandfather fled Ukraine to come here. He walked through *snow* and *ice* and over *mountains* just to catch a train to Germany, and then he had to sit on that train for *weeks*. And he had nothing. Crusts of old bread and cheese. He had one potato he would peel every other day, and he would let the skin sit in his mouth for *hours* just so he could suck in every last vitamin. Could you imagine that?"

Emily was almost certain her grandmother was lying to her, but she loved the way she was telling the story, the way her voice giddily rose and fell, almost drunkenly, and yet her voice was crisp, and she articulated her words beautifully.

"Would you like that, kiddo? An uncooked potato skin for dinner?" Her grandmother poked her in her delicate belly, and Emily pulled away and laughed.

"No potato skins for me, thanks," said Emily.

"And after all that, he made his way to Germany, took one look at all the *mishegas* there, and got on a boat and spent four more weeks crowded together with a bunch of other Jews trying to get the hell out of there, and the whole time he was *still peeling that one potato*."

"Was it a big potato to start?" said Emily, stifling laughter.

"It was a pretty big potato, I have to admit," said

her grandmother. "But still! To only eat potato for such a long time, that's not that much fun, right?"

Emily nodded somberly.

"So by the time he got to America, he was just skin and bones. He barely made it alive." Her grandmother's voice started to quiver. "And he lost a lot of his friends and family along the way. You should have heard him talk about it. I'm sorry you didn't get to know him like I did. He was a really nice man. He wrote beautiful letters."

Emily took her grandmother's arm with her one good arm. They had one more lap to walk.

"But here is the point, Emily. Are you ready for the point?"

"Yes," said Emily.

"Even after traveling all that way, and even on a diet composed almost exclusively of potato skin, all that for months and months, your great-grandfather still showed up in America with a full head of hair," she said triumphantly. "So I don't know what the hell is wrong with your father."

"Me neither," said Emily.

"I'm hungry. Are you hungry?" said her grandmother.

"Starving," said Emily.

"You must be famished after all that exercise," said her grandmother.

"Let's eat," said Emily.

"How do you feel about Chinese food?" said her grandmother.

How Emily felt about Chinese food was that it was mostly greasy but that she liked shrimp dumplings and that anything was better than what was being served in her house as of late, which was mainly (really, only) vegetables, sometimes raw, sometimes steamed, sometimes, if they were really lucky, stir-fried with just a hint of oil, and all this gross tofu that felt like cottage cheese in her mouth (cottage cheese for breakfast: also gross), all these meals designed to keep them trim and fit and elevate their levels of health, and to keep the diabetes bug away as if it were something you could catch rather than earn by eating gallons and gallons of junk food for years and years, which was clearly what her grandmother had done. But the way she felt that day was that one egg roll wouldn't hurt, and there was part of her that was embarrassed to be at the high-school track, like she was some poser pretending she was already a student there.

So she and her grandmother sped home— suddenly they could both move extremely quickly—and hopped into the car and drove for a while, back past the high school, the giant digital marquee alluringly blinking in front of it about prom, baseball playoffs, the math club's bake sale, the future, Emily's future, taller, older, wiser, bigger, smarter, brighter, you are almost here, down roads she had never been down without her mother and father, except for school trips downtown, past the Chuck E. Cheese where she and her brother had a birthday party one year, past stores where she shopped with her mother sometimes (the Jewel grocery store where her mother shopped in a pinch when she didn't have time to make the trek to Whole Foods, a greeting-card shop because *It's always important to send thank-you notes,* a beauty-supply store where her mother bought expensive shampoos and face creams for cheap, the sporting-goods store where they stocked up on soccer shoes and shorts every spring, that mega-Target for school supplies but never clothes, her mother wouldn't let her be caught dead in Target clothes), past roads that went to nowhere in particular as far as Emily was concerned, though she supposed people lived this way and that, even if she didn't know *who* exactly, until her grandmother pulled in to a dirty little strip mall and up to a Chinese restaurant.

Through the window Emily could see that her Aunt Robin was already there, a pinched expression on her face, several manila folders in front of her on the table, and a glass of wine (Aunt Robin did like her wine, that was *known* in the family) in front of those. Her aunt was her favorite person in the world, behind her father (the most reasonable man on the planet) and her brother (wimpy or not, he was one half of the whole) and occasionally a friend at school who had proved herself to not be a total waste of time. Her aunt would probably be number one on the list if Emily saw her more often, but Robin made herself scarce most of the time, off in the city, which lent her a certain appeal as well, an air of mystery and cool, even if deep down Emily knew there were much technically cooler people in the universe. But still, Robin spoke to her as if she were an equal or at least not a child, and always had for as long as Emily could remember, and Emily had appreciated it (now more than ever) even though she had never said it out loud to her aunt.

Inside the restaurant Robin gave her a genuine smile, which then turned to a sour glance at Emily's grandmother.

"Got yourself your very own human shield, huh, old lady?" said Robin. Then she stood up from the table and hugged her niece, and they kissed on each cheek like ladies did in the movies, French ladies, or fashionable older ladies who lived in New York City.

"I don't know what you're talking about," said Emily's grandmother, who lowered herself into a seat, Robin gently assisting her. "What's wrong with me spending time with my two favorite girls?"

"There's nothing wrong with it," said Robin. "I just thought we were going to discuss a few things here." She ran her hands over the manila folders sitting in front of her.

"You can talk about whatever you want to talk

about," said Emily boldly. "I probably already know what you're going to talk about." She actually had little idea of what was going on, but she could only imagine that it was about her grandmother being sick, because everything was always about her grandmother being sick; it had been for months. Longer? Longer.

Robin exchanged a dark look with Edie, and then said, "You want to be the one explaining this to her mother?"

"Why don't you go wash your hands before dinner?" said Edie.

Emily made a bitchy little noise, a noise she had only recently started practicing and one that would get much, much better with age, but she got up resignedly and wandered through the empty restaurant, which she finally noticed was sort of cute, with its weathered wooden tables and sweet little glass bowls of pink flowers, and back toward the bathroom, passing the kitchen doors, from which wild notes of jazz emanated, and she wondered where she was exactly, because it did not feel quite like anywhere she had been before.

In the bathroom, red, dimly lit, lavender-drenched, she used her one good arm to wash herself, her palms and her fingers, with hot water, and then her forehead, her cheeks, her chin, her neck, behind her ears, little drops dripping down onto her shirt. More soap and water, this time lifting her shirt up and splashing and scrubbing under her arms. Sometimes she felt like she could never get clean enough, but she didn't know why.

As it turned out, she felt that way because her mother had taught her to feel that way, and she'll figure that out eventually, in college, in New York, when her freshman-year roommate, a Spanish girl from Barcelona named Agnes, studying film just like she is, asks her why she is always washing up and Emily says, without even thinking, "Men like a clean girl," and then says quickly, "Oh, God, I sound just like my mother, how terrible," and the Spanish girl says, "And your mother maybe isn't even so right about this." Later Agnes will take her to a party in a loft building in Brooklyn, on the waterfront, and they will stand on the roof together holding hands amid other young, excited people like themselves, sweating, smoking, drinking, smiling, feeling extremely sexy, and they'll look at the city in the distance, lit up magnificently, the length of it blowing their minds. They will try to figure out which bridge is which, and they will confuse the Manhattan Bridge with the Brooklyn Bridge. There will be a young bearded man playing cover songs on an accordion, and all the girls will want to sleep with him, except for the girls who want to sleep with the other girls. And then Emily will remember a story her aunt had told her about living in Brooklyn a long time ago, and hating it there, the noise, the dirt, the anger, and fleeing the city for home, Chicago, and never looking back, and all Emily can think is: *She must have gone to the wrong Brooklyn. Because I never want to go home again.*

But at age twelve the most important thing was whatever was right in front of her face, in this case herself, her eyes, the same eyes as her grandmother's and her aunt's, the sweet genetic strain tugging her back out the bathroom door and toward her family. Her grandmother and aunt were probably discussing great and important truths that would be relevant to Emily's being successful in her existence as an older (though not old) and wiser person. She arrived at the table just as Robin was tucking one envelope back into her bag.

"What was that?" Emily said breathlessly.

"Paperwork," said her grandmother, who, if she had been shaken at all, had quickly recovered.

"Are you guys having, like, a family secret?" said Emily. "Ooh, scary." There were still two folders left.

"Smart-ass," said Robin.

"Where does she get it from, I wonder," said her grandmother, amused. "Do you want anything special?" She handed Emily a menu.

"I only like shrimp dumplings," said Emily.

"This place is pretty good," said her grandmother. "You should try more than that just to try it."

"Why should I eat if I don't want to?" said Emily.

"For the experience," said her grandmother firmly.

How's that experience working for you? Emily thought, and then blushed at her own cruelty, even if it was only internal.

Her aunt must have intercepted her thoughts in some sort of familial shortwave exchange, because she snapped, "She doesn't have to eat if she doesn't want to." Robin drank the rest of her wine in one gulp, and she ran her hands across the tops of the folders. More quietly, she said, "Just get her the dumplings."

"It's not a big deal either way," said Emily. "I'll eat whatever."

"Get what you want," said Robin.

Emily looked at her gratefully. She appreciated the protection, which she had never felt like she needed until that moment, at least not from her grandmother. In a few years, her aunt would again protect her when the shit really started to go down between Emily and her mother; there was screaming and yelling and one hair-pulling incident, and so it was decided that on certain weekends Emily would spend some time with her schoolteacher aunt and her boyfriend in their apartment downtown, because clearly Emily, who was so *bright* and so *creative* (and yet so good at math, a fact everyone always ignored), needed a wider cultural perspective, visits to galleries and museums and vintage stores and bookstores and independent movie theaters and so forth, and those visits once a month helped clear everyone's head, her mother's, her father's, Emily's, and those visits would have continued had her aunt not had the breakdown that one night, too much to drink, too sad, a lost baby in her belly that no one had known about except for her boyfriend, and it had been too much for her aunt to handle, mourning this thing she had known for only a few weeks, not even a baby, just an idea of a baby, and it had devastated her so much, too much, and it had scared Emily, to see someone who couldn't stop crying for so long into the night and through the next morning until her father could come pick her up, just one urgent phone call away. "You're welcome back whenever you like, as soon as she gets better," said Robin's boyfriend, Daniel, red-faced and sad himself, but by the time she was ready, after the brief hospital stay and the many therapy sessions, and the stopping and starting and stopping again of drinking, Emily was long gone to college.

"The dumplings are delicious," said her grandmother, embarrassed, staring deeply at the menu. "You can't go wrong with the dumplings." Her grandmother ordered a few dishes from a cool-looking waitress who was maybe her aunt's age but looked younger with her purple-striped hair and high-legged lace-up leather boots and punky miniskirt. "And whatever else you think is good," she said. "But I wanted my granddaughter to try those dishes."

"Your granddaughter!" the waitress squealed, and then rushed to Emily's side, extending her hand, and Emily wondered why the waitress was so happy to see her. "Of course, look at all of you, three peas in a pod. The same eyes," she said. It was true: They all had the same dark eyes; Emily's were not damaged yet, though, no wounds burned deep within her, not like with the two women.

"Emily, this is Anna," said her grandmother.

Emily was still looking at the waitress's hand, specifically her nails, which were painted a sparkly purple color.

"She's a friend of mine," said her grandmother. "Go on, don't be rude. Shake her hand."

Emily reached out and shook the waitress's hand.

"I like your nail polish," she said, and she felt completely lame, but she had never been introduced to a waitress in her life. She knew her family and her friends at school and the people at the synagogue and some of her neighbors and her parents' friends and some random distant relatives, but people who worked out in the world, the people who served you at various stores and restaurants, were not people you befriended, not because you were better than they were (or they were worse than you), but because . . . she didn't know why because. Because they didn't quite exist for her yet. Maybe, just then, they started to exist.

"I've got the bottle in back," said Anna. "I can grab it for you, it's no trouble."

"Aren't you just so lovely," said her grand-mother. "After we eat, of course."

Seven plates of food arrived soon after, plus three bowls of rice, but Emily ignored most of it, keeping her eye on the folders, and her aunt, who was watching her grandmother eat, while her grandmother ignored her and piled food on her own plate and ate and ate and ate, she didn't stop for nothing, head down, chopsticks in one hand, a spoon in the other, like it was a contest, like she was in a race, but it never seemed like she was going to finish, like her grandmother could eat forever and never get full. *This is how you got that way,* thought Emily, who ate only three dumplings, even though they were delicious, dewy and plump and slightly sweet, because she was beginning to feel sick watching her grandmother. She looked again at her aunt's face, and realized she was sick, too. Only the waitress, Anna, wasn't sick. She was cheerful, clearing the plates as her grandmother emptied them with efficiency. She was the only one who didn't know. Emily wondered if anyone was planning on telling her. She bet Anna would want to know.

With the post-dinner green tea (and *just one more* glass of wine for her aunt, she *probably wouldn't even finish it*) came the bottle of purple polish, and Emily quietly busied herself with her nails, dabbing and blowing delicately, working awkwardly with the cast, while her aunt opened the first folder.

"We're going to talk about your grandmother's health for a little bit," said Robin.

"Maybe we shouldn't do that in front of her," said her grandmother.

"Is it going to bum you out?" said Robin.

"The whole thing is already a bummer," said Emily. Her grandmother started to cry. "Don't cry," said Emily, and then she started to cry, and so did Robin. Anna walked up with three dishes of ice cream, made a small, horrified expression with her mouth, and then walked away, silver dishes still in hand.

"Everyone cut it out," Robin said finally, dabbing her eyes with her napkin.

"It's going to be fine, honey," said her grandmother, who did not stop the tears dripping from her face. "Come here, *bubbeleh*." She extended her arms toward Emily, who slung her one good arm around her grandmother's torso and clung tightly.

"Breathe," said Robin. They did. They all breathed separately. They all breathed collectively. "Now, let's get down to business."

She opened the top folder. It was full of brochures. *Spas, retreats, resorts.*

"Fat farms," murmured her grandmother.

"You have to start somewhere," said Robin.

"I'm not going anywhere," said the older woman. "I don't want to leave my family right now."

"I've also got some information on nutritionists," said Robin. She pulled out a single slick sheet of paper that had a picture of a buff, smiling man with enormous teeth that somehow seemed whiter than the paper they were printed on. "This guy is supposed to be one of the best trainers in Chicago, and he specializes in cases like yours. He's in the suburbs on Tuesdays and Fridays."

"I already walk around the track almost every day," said her grandmother.

"You're going to need more than the track," said Robin.

"I'm doing the best I can," said her grandmother.

"*This* is the best you can?" said Robin angrily, motioning to the now-empty table.

"I like it here," whispered her grandmother. "These are my friends. You can't make me give up my friends."

Emily suddenly felt nervous; the humanity, the rawness of emotions of those she loved and revered, it was a lot to handle. She didn't want to know this yet. She said suddenly, "What's in the other folder?"

The two women looked at her. Robin smoothed her hand nervously over the table. "Maybe this is too much," she said. Emily reached out her good hand and quickly pulled the folder toward her, then flipped it open. Weight-loss surgery. Staples and tubes. "That's probably not for right now," said her aunt. "It could be for later this year." Robin paled, and rubbed her hands along the sides of her face. "It's not ideal. It's not entirely guaranteed, and any time you go in for surgery, you're putting yourself at risk." Robin could no longer look at her mother or her niece. "It's a way to go. It's not the way I would go. But it is a way to go. It's something to think about." She lurched forward and clutched at her mother. "Can't you just stop, please, stop, Mom, please?"

"Yes, please," said Emily.

Her grandmother squeezed her daughter's hands and released them. She closed both folders and laid them on the seat next to her, nodding to herself. "I promise you I will read all this tonight," she said.

"I'm going to call you tomorrow," said Robin. "First thing."

"Good," said her mother. "It is always a pleasure to hear from you." She finally wiped at her eyes with her napkin, then turned to Emily and said, "Have you ever seen a real restaurant kitchen before? Come on, come meet the chef."

The two of them walked back to the double

kitchen doors, her grandmother knocking on one and then poking her head inside. "Yoo-hoo," she said. "Can we come in?" Emily stuck her head in, too, and Anna huddled in the corner of the gleaming white kitchen with an older Chinese man, wrinkled, tall, stooped, and worried-looking.

"Of course you can," said the man. "Of course, of course." He waved them in. "You are okay?" he asked her grandmother.

"Yes, we're just a bunch of emotional gals," she said. "It runs in the family."

"Three peas in a pod," Anna said.

"Three weepy peas," said her grandmother. "Emily, meet Anna's dad, Kenneth. This is his place. He's the chef."

The man, this stranger, though maybe not a strange man, but definitely not her grandfather, came toward her grandmother, took her hand, squeezed her hand, brushed it against his cheek, kissed it lightly, lowered it, leaned toward her, kissed her on her cheek, kissed her again on her cheek, then kissed her on the corner of her mouth, stopping just short of a full-mouth kiss, but it was not necessary, he had already done enough to show his intentions toward her grandmother, and when Emily looked at her grandmother's face, peachy and flushed and so clearly delighted, then watched as her grandmother leaned forward toward this man and fully, blatantly, kissed him on his lips, like she didn't even care that Emily was standing right there (with *so many questions*), Emily knew that there was no way her grandmother was ever going to go away to any fat farm or ever stop eating all that Chinese food, and Emily could not blame her, because if she had a man who looked at her like Kenneth looked at her grandmother and wanted to cook for her and kiss her all over her hands and cheeks and lips, she would stay with him forever and ever, until the day she died.

Middlestein in Love

OH, BEVERLY, THOUGHT Richard Middlestein, daydreaming again of his first crush since sometime in the late 1960s, right before he met his wife (his *estranged* wife, to be precise) and gave up his life completely (or incompletely, as he had been thinking lately) to a woman he no longer loved. But here, now, he felt, as genuinely as he was capable of feeling, that he had a second chance at love with Beverly, formerly of the UK until a Chicagoan stole her away twenty years earlier, red-haired (still natural, even in her late fifties; this bowled him over), plump-cheeked, bold but not brassy, practical, smart, witty, clever even, half Jewish but on the right side, with big, batty, beautiful green eyes, lovely Beverly who made perfect sense all the time and had a certain order to her life that he would like to apply to his own.

Beverly! Who gave him the time of day only once a week, if he was lucky, leaving his e-mails unreplied to, his phone calls unanswered, until he finally got the hint, she was not a woman who could be crowded or pushed, she did everything on her own time in her own way, she carried herself through this life with dignity, and he wanted a little of that for himself. Whatever she knew, he wanted to know.

Beverly! The lovely widow of a fantastic man, a kind ophthalmologist, who'd left her set for life. (She had a lot more than Middlestein in the bank, that much he knew.) Beverly, childless (no baggage, none whatsoever!), but who still loved children. Beverly, who liked to do *things*, lots of things, go to the movies, go to the theater, watch footy on weekend mornings, go for drives along the lake, go for bike rides, eat nice meals, have elegant dinner parties, all these things that did not involve walking too much, many of them mainly related to sitting, which was perfect for Richard and his not-so-great knees.

Beverly! So precious with her British accent, in her soccer jerseys, hanging out in that ancient, smoke-stained pub with the awful breakfasts (shriveled, ruddy sausages; Middlestein had been unable to force himself to even take a bite) with her expat girlfriends, cheering for Tottenham, even though (or because) they were a bunch of losers. Once she had let him come and sit with her for a match early on a Saturday morning, and they had all cheered and roared (this year, at last, Tottenham had been winning), and sipped Guinness (for her and her friends) and Bloody Marys (for him), and afterward she had listened to his problems and, miracle of all miracles, *solved them*, or some of them anyway, the early-morning alcohol perhaps infusing her with a shocking clarity, and in retrospect he became convinced she could even see into his soul. And now he waited to be invited every week—he knew he couldn't just crash her party, that would be the surest way to make her lose interest in him—but she hadn't asked him since, settling instead for quiet little dinners, which were satisfying in their own way, but there was something about the moment they had both experienced during that early-morning drunk, how her hand had fluttered to his hands and once to his cheek, the directness of her gaze, which seemed to melt with his in the dusty streaks of sunlight vibrating in their booth; he hadn't felt that same connection with her since, and he knew if he could just have one more morning with her, if she would grace him again with that same energy, they would be able to move beyond the gentle pecks on the cheek she gave him when she bid him good-bye in the parking lot of whatever restaurant they had dined in—too briefly!—that night.

It was Beverly who suggested he write a letter to his daughter-in-law, Rachelle, asking for permission to once again be a participant in the lives of his grandchildren. "Your son can't help you," she said. "He can't speak on your behalf. This decision came from her. You have to go directly to the source." Dust sparkling all around her head. "And a phone call won't do, nor will an

217

e-mail. Don't be a lazy man. Write her a proper letter." She ran "lazy man" together as if it were one word, as if it were an actual thing, a term she had created herself, because Beverly had the power to create new words. "Pour your heart out on that paper, tell her how much you love and miss those children, put it in an envelope, stick a stamp on it, and then mail it."

To spend time with Josh and Emily is my heart's desire, he wrote. He was starting to sound like Beverly, which was not such a bad thing.

"Then what?"

"Give her a week."

Sure enough, a week later, there was Rachelle standing in front of him at the pharmacy, a prescription in her hand, herself with a slight case of the stink eye.

"I'm not completely sure about any of this," she said. She handed him the prescription; it was for Lopressor, a heart medication, and it was for his someday-ex-wife. If that action was meant to stab him slightly in the chest, it worked.

"About what?" he said.

Say your piece just the once and then let her do all the talking, Beverly had said. He had known that already; he had some understanding of what it meant to contend with an angry woman.

"I don't want them thinking your behavior, your actions, are excused. Because they are not."

"Of course not," he said. He wouldn't even

begin to justify his actions to her, leaving his sick, emotionally unstable, diabetes-and heart-disease- and who-knows-what-else-ridden wife, because he knew she didn't want to hear it. Even though in his head it made sense.

Beverly understood! Beverly was the first person he had met who got it perfectly, Beverly with her mean drunk of a father, a military man crushed by time as a prisoner of war during World War II. "I had my sympathies for the man," she said. "We all did." Richard nodded. Their generation, his and Beverly's, they all had family, and they all had heard stories from the war growing up.

And then Beverly added—and was this the moment his heart skipped for her?—with a downtrodden yet dreamy voice: *You never know what's worse with the angry ones, watching them live, or watching them die.*

"With the b'nai mitzvah approaching," continued Rachelle, "and with all the family in town, Benny and I want you in attendance of course. And we still would like you to recite the kiddush, obviously." His daughter-in-law had an insistent formality, spine as straight as a rod, every hair in place, her nails a pearly pink, ironed, pressed, tightly controlled. She reminded him of the average Zoloft or Prozac customer. (He was no doctor, so he would never say anything like that to his son, but she seemed like she might *benefit*.)

"I'll be there," said Richard. "With bells on."

"Don't wear bells," said Rachelle.

"I would never wear bells," said Richard. "It's an expression."

"I know it's an expression," she said, suddenly flushed and flustered, her neck delicately purpling. *This is hard for her,* he thought. *Why?* In that moment of weakness, he made a grab for the gold.

"I would like to see them before the b'nai mitzvah," he said. "I could take them to services on Friday night? Or next week?"

It was Beverly who encouraged him to suggest taking the grandkids to Friday-night services. If these kids were so important to him—they were; Richard practically shouted this—then he needed to think *outside the box,* this last phrase she relished dramatically. Sure, it was more fun to go to the movies or shopping or get pizza, but he was probably not allowed to be having fun yet with his two gorgeous grandchildren, not in his daughter-in-law's eyes anyway. Friday-night services weren't about having fun; they were about being contemplative. The subtler point was (and she was right, Richard could not deny it) that he was not an out-of-the-box thinker. He was completely in the box. (What was so wrong with the box? He had felt this way his entire life.) But by leaving his wife at the age of sixty, he had hurtled himself out there, out into the universe, out of the goddamn box. And if he had not done so, he never would have met Beverly. So it was up to him to do whatever it took to stay there.

"Let me talk to Benny," Rachelle said, and her skin returned to its normal (though possibly tanning-creamed) golden color. He had placed the power in her hands once again, given her something to decide upon. *That's where she likes to be,* he thought. *On top.* And his mind briefly traveled to a sexual moment, not with his daughter-in-law, of course (although maybe she was nearby, down the hall or in a doorway watching), but with Beverly, vibrant-eyed, sensible yet magical, unavailable yet somehow still within reach, Beverly, his hands reaching up to her, and she waved her body back and forth on top of him, a greeting, an introduction of two bodies to each other, an explosive exchange of a specific kind of information. Beverly grinding on his dick, Beverly straddling his face, Beverly all over him all day and night long.

Beverly!

At shul the following week—of course Rachelle had said yes to Richard's request; there was no way she could say no to a grandfather sincerely wanting to take his children to synagogue, there was certainly a rule about that somewhere in some daughter-in-law handbook—Richard meandered lightly down the main aisle of the sanctuary, his two grandchildren, their tongues struck by silence since the moment they'd gotten into the car, shuffling behind him. He waved to the Cohns and the Grodsteins and the Weinmans and the Frankens, all the couples he had come up together with for the last twenty, thirty, nearly forty years. They had all gone to each other's children's bar mitzvahs and weddings and anniversary parties and thank God no funerals yet, but he supposed they would be attending those, too, until there was no one left.

How would that feel? To be the last one standing? Who was going to make it to the end? Would it be Albert Weinman, who swam every morning and golfed every weekend and ate egg-white everything? Or Lauren Franken, who'd already had a double mastectomy, and joked that she'd gotten the hard part out of the way early and it was all smooth sailing ahead? Surely it wouldn't be Bobby Grodstein, the way he smoked those cigars after dinner.

He allowed himself to consider his practically-ex-wife, her supersized existence, the secret eating late at night (every night he could hear her opening cupboards and packages and crunching crunching crunching, echoing through the quietude of their home, their street, their town, their world, but he had given up on trying to stop her), the twice-weekly trips to Costco (even though he knew where all the food had gone, he couldn't help but wonder out loud to her every single time she went, "What do you need?"), the flesh stacked upon flesh stacked upon flesh. No, she would not outlive him.

Would it be Richard himself? He worked out a few times a week, not as hard as he could, sure, but those knees of his . . . His blood pressure was good, his cholesterol was a little high, but nothing he couldn't manage with Lipitor. He took vitamins. He ate his RDA of fruits and vegetables, sometimes even much, much more than the RDA. During his last checkup, his doctor had given him a friendly swat on the arm before he left the room, clipboard in hand, and promised he would live a long life. "There's no reason you couldn't live till one hundred," is what he said.

Would he want to make it that long? Would he want everyone he knew to be gone? Except for his family, they'd probably outlive him: Benny, who he knew would forgive him eventually even if he had lost respect for him, and his sullen daughter, Robin, who was already too busy to visit him while he was still a fully functioning human being—what about when he was old and decrepit in a nursing home? He'd off himself before that happened. He'd off himself before he was wearing diapers. He knew it. He could prescribe himself the exact mixture he would need to send himself to a faraway dreamland, never to wake up again. For decades he had been facing the adult-diaper section in his pharmacy, studying the people who purchased them, their slow, miserable shuffle, imagining he could see right through their clothes to what was underneath. Your needs at the beginning of your life and at the end of your life were exactly the same. But Richard Middlestein was no baby; he was a man. (He felt like pounding his chest right there in the middle of the temple. Beverly!) He'd live until the day he was ready to die.

If his grandkids didn't kill him first.

Because there were Josh and Emily, all three of them now seated in a prominent position close to the aisle and near the front of the room, just four rows from the bimah, and even though they were huddled over slightly, it was clear that they had their cell phones out *and they were texting.* (Middlestein thought texting was the same as Morse code, and the more people texted, the closer America came to being a nation at war. "Think about it," he'd told Beverly, poking his index finger on his temple.) He leaned across Josh and squeezed one of Emily's hands—the hand that was tap-tapping—and rested his arm across Josh's lap, and then, with as much restraint as possible, because he did not want to alert the Cohns and the Grodsteins and the Weinmans and the Frankens, all of whom were seated two rows behind him, that his grandchildren had apparently been *raised by wolves,* he said, "Put those away." Josh, simple, scrawny, sweet-faced, looked instantly terrified and shoved his phone into his back pocket, but Emily was another story. Emily was so much like her grandmother and her aunt—at least in appearance, but Middlestein suspected it went much further than that—she was practically marked by the devil. She gave him a mean look, and was precariously close to opening her mouth, and what she might say, and at what volume she might say it, he could only imagine. If she were truly like her grandmother, it would be just loud enough so that everyone around them could hear but not so loud that it could be considered inappropriate. Nothing to ruin anyone's reputation over anyway. Not like everyone hadn't lost it on their spouse at one time or another.

But young Emily did not yell. She merely whispered, "I'm not done yet," and then, in perhaps her most offensive act of the evening (and there were a few yet to come), shook his hand off hers with vigor. Middlestein pulled his hand back, stunned by her aggression. Josh turned to her openmouthed but did not say a thing, closed his mouth, turned away, faced forward, opened his mouth again, and turned toward her, and the two of them stared at each other, and then—this was the part that crushed Middlestein, that made him realize that it was possible there was no one left in this family he had a decent relationship with (And was it his fault? He had nearly convinced himself it wasn't.)—Josh let off a short, staccato laugh, as if he were trying to control it but could not.

Once he had bathed these little babies. Once he had bounced them on his knee and ran his fingers through their soft curls. These were going to be the children he would never argue with, never punish, whose curfew he would never have to worry about. He would never have to spank them. He would never have to disappoint them. All he had to do was spoil them rotten, overspend on every birthday and Hanukkah just to see their eager smiles. Now they revered their iPhones above religious decorum and thought he was a schmuck because he'd left his wife. Now they didn't give a shit what he thought.

Middlestein was devastated throughout the entire service. He could barely bring himself to sing the Shema, which had always been such a soothing prayer for him, a proclamation of his faith. It had always been so good to believe in something. Now he was distracted by the little miss down the row, with her eye rolling and sighing and the loudest page flipping this side of the Mississippi, her brother choking in his laughter, the Cohns and the Grodsteins and the Weinmans and the Frankens giving him rueful glances. It wasn't enough that he had abandoned his wife, now he had ill-behaved grandchildren too? Shameful. He was shamed.

Once he had counted their fingers and toes, just

to make sure they were all there. Their nails were like dewdrops. *This little piggy went to market, this little piggy stayed home.*

He sighed and closed his eyes and tried to achieve bliss: Beverly! What did her toes look like? He knew she got a manicure (and a pedicure) once a week from the Polish girls in the same mini-mall that housed his pharmacy. She strolled in afterward, her nails glowing coral, afraid to fish out her wallet from her purse. "I always end up chipping," she said with that adorable British accent of hers, offering her purse to Middlestein. As he roamed through her sunglasses and cell phone and lipstick and checkbook and a paperback novel, on the cover of which was a dark-skinned man with bright blue eyes against some sort of Middle Eastern backdrop (it looked *smart*), a package of Wrigley's peppermint gum (a classic and elegant choice if one had to chew gum), and a dozen pens (freebies from local businesses, he had a box of them himself that he handed out to customers, all bearing the Middlestein Drugs logo), he was touched by the intimacy of the moment, even if she was a complete stranger. There were three quarters at the bottom of her purse, and a tube of ChapStick. A plastic comb, also bearing the logo of a local business. Did she just say yes every time someone handed her something? Was she too nice to say no? Nobody needed that many pens.

She was buying a greeting card, for a college graduation; on the cover there was a young man wearing a mortarboard in a hot air balloon, and on the inside, opposite a flap to hold a check, it read "Congratulations on moving on up in the world!" It was a dumb sentiment, but he carried only five different kinds of college-graduation cards in his display. (He had been trying to phase them out since 1998 but couldn't bring himself to throw them away.) He suddenly wanted nothing more than to impress this British beauty, and all he had to offer were decade-old greeting cards.

He waved the card at her. "Mazel tov," he said. "Your son?"

"Nephew. Michigan State." She blew on her nails.

"That's a gorgeous color on those nails," he said.

She pulled her hands away from her face and cocked her head as she stared at them. "But it's a bit bright, isn't it?"

"Nah, it's perfect," he said. "You should always wear that color."

He pulled a five-dollar bill out of her wallet.

"I don't like to be too flashy," she said.

"Add a little sparkle to your day, there's nothing wrong with that," he said.

She straightened herself and stared at him meaningfully. "Truer words were never spoken," she said. And then she collapsed slightly. "Life is so dull sometimes." She gave him a wistful but (he was almost positive) flirty smile. "It's as if I can hear the clock ticking off the minutes of the day."

"I can't imagine a woman like you, with nails like those, would ever be bored."

"I keep myself busy," she said. "I have hobbies." She said "hobbies" with a bit of spite. As much as he had hated his ex-wife's ire and venom, he did find a woman with an edge extremely attractive; they were so fearless. "But lately I've found myself just waiting for something to happen."

Did this gorgeous, witty, well-read, nicely groomed, age-appropriate, mostly organized woman really just walk into his pharmacy and lay out an invitation for him to flirt with her? Had he done anything good that day to deserve this moment?

"I noticed there's no ring on that finger," said Middlestein.

"I noticed there's no ring on your finger either," she said.

Ante up, Middlestein.

Down the aisle Emily flung herself into a coughing fit, a grimacing Josh patting her on the back, and then Beverly's smile gave way to a vision of his any-second-now-ex-wife. She had been hovering somewhere in the back of his mind and then pushed her way to the front, knocking Beverly over until she returned, timidly, to a dark space out of frame. Edie said nothing, she just stood there, her hands in fists, her presence enormous. Everyone in the temple sang, and so did Richard, and he looked at his grandchildren, and Josh was singing, and Emily had her arms crossed and was staring into space. An angry young girl. She looked at her grandfather, sneered, and turned back toward nothing in particular. Richard faced forward, folded his hands together, rested his forehead on them, and began to pray on behalf of his (if he had to be honest with himself now that he was in an actual conversation with God here) long-drawn-out-legal-battle-until-she's-his-ex-wife. Because she was sick, she was very, very sick, in the head, in the heart, in the flesh, and even though he could not watch over her anymore, it never hurt to ask God for a little help. Here he was, in his house of worship, asking for help for her. Because now that he was really being honest, he'd give up Beverly in a second if he knew that it would heal Edie. But he knew that nothing would make her better. That's what he knew that no one else did, not his daughter or his son or that little grimacing monkey two seats down. That Edie didn't care if she lived or died.

Middlestein almost felt like he might cry, and where better to do it but here, under the watchful eye of God? He had seen so many people cry over the years in synagogue, in this long life of his, particularly during the Kaddish. He was born a few years after the Holocaust had ended, but it seemed like it dragged on for years, the wailing and the moaning, gradually fading to tender streams of tears accompanied by a choked-up sound, the sadness trapped in the heart and the chest and the throat, resolving, years after the fact, into just a whimper, for some faraway soul. (Could they even remember what their lost loved ones looked like anymore?) Then there was Vietnam. There was cancer. Heart attacks and strokes and car accidents. A surprising amount of cliff-diving accidents. (Six.) Suicides, hushed. Old age. Bankruptcy. Runaway children. Hands clenched across the heart, as if the white-hot force between the palms could make a miracle happen. If one believed in miracles. So many wars over the years, sons and daughters came and went. Pray for them, and pray for Israel while you're at it, too. (Everyone always should be praying for Israel.) Hold on to hope. Hold on to love. Hold on to your family, because they won't always be around.

Where better to cry?

But where worse to cry than under the watchful eye of the Cohns and the Grodsteins and the Weinmans and the Frankens? They didn't need to know how bad it was. He didn't want them talking about him later in their living rooms, over a nightcap of fat-free snacks. Worrying or judging, he didn't know which, and it didn't matter; either way would make him feel weak and helpless, and even after all these years of being in each other's lives, what did they know anyway? *They didn't know anything about him.*

Or to cry in front of Emily, who was now slumped on her brother's shoulder, looking in profile a little dreamy, less like the Middlestein women and more like her mother, her petite chin, the smooth drop of her forehead, the pink swell of her lips, the furious blaze of her eyes temporarily dampened, as if she had pulled herself deep underwater, and was holding her breath until she turned blue. She must have felt him staring at her: she suddenly shook her head, and the eyes were relit. She had remembered she was supposed to be mad at him. No, he would not cry in front of Emily either.

After the services were over, he hustled the two children, his hands in an exceedingly firm grip on the backs of both of their necks, out the door, past the wall of gold leaves embossed with the names of donors—his was up near the top, because he was one of the first, although it had been a long time since he had given any sizable amount of money, *what with this economy*—all of them forming the long limbs of a tree, reaching up and outward as if they were holding up the synagogue. He didn't stop to chitchat with anyone, just a nod and a "Good *Shabbos*," making a hapless, dog-eyed expression toward the children, as if to say, *It's not me, it's them.*

Outside, in the late-spring evening, the crack of summer heat curling at its edges, as they dodged the cars pulling up curbside to pick up the elderly, then mixed in with all those people filled with prayer and joy, the women in high heels, the men in their suit coats (no ties necessary during the warmer weather), the children running and giggling, released at last from sitting still, everyone immersed in that post-shul glow, he almost let himself forget that his grandchildren had engaged in such subversive behavior. He was, in fact, ready to forgive them, until Emily said, loudly, "I'm so glad *that's* over."

"It's over when I tell you it's over," said Middlestein. "You're lucky I don't make you go back in there and have a talk with the rabbi himself about how God feels about texting during shul. He'd have a thing or two to say to you."

"We didn't want to come, you should know that," said Emily.

"Shut up, Emily," said Josh.

"You shut up," said Emily.

"I think he knows that already," said Josh.

Middlestein released his hands from their backs, which had started to sweat, and pulled out his keys from his suit-coat pocket, pressing the unlock-door button even though they were still at least a dozen rows from his car. He passed Josh, he passed Emily, he passed the Weinmans, headed, as they did every week, to a Shabbat dinner with Al's elderly mother at her nursing home in Oak Park. He walked and walked through the streaming crowds until he was at his car, and he got in, and he sat, and he waited for those little sons of bitches to get there.

Josh got in first, Emily pausing with her hand on the door, starting a staring competition with her grandfather that she almost instantly comprehended—he could see her bite her lip—she was never going to win. *Don't you understand,* he wanted to say, *I invented the staring contest? Don't you understand that, as far as you know, I invented* everything?

She got into the car, the front seat, and pulled herself as far away from him as she could.

Years ago, seventeen, maybe eighteen by now, Middlestein sat in this same parking lot with his daughter, Robin, but in a different car—was it the Accord then?—and he was just as furious with her as he was with Emily now. It was a month before Robin's bat mitzvah, and she still hadn't memorized her haftorah. The cantor had called them in for an emergency meeting, only Robin hadn't realized that's what it was, or maybe she didn't care, because—if it was possible—she was even more sullen than Emily was now. Robin these days was a confident though still difficult woman, but at the age of thirteen she was awkward and chubby, with a head of hair like a mushroom cloud, and cranky because of all that.

Middlestein had adored her anyway. She was the youngest. She was trickier than Benny. She would retreat and attack quickly, a limber boxer. He never had a handle on her once she learned how to talk back. And there she was talking back to Cantor Rubin, then a young man, bearded, barrel-chested, a new recruit to the synagogue (Middlestein had offered to give him a discount at the pharmacy, but Rubin had never shown up, not in all these years, a slight insult if he had to admit it), giving him lip while he tried to explain calmly that if she just worked with the tape every night, one hour a night, he was confident she would have her haftorah down by her bat mitzvah. And Robin dryly said, "Can't we just play the tape instead and I'll lip-sync it? No one's going to be paying attention anyway." If it was a joke, it wasn't funny. If she was serious, then why was Middlestein shelling out twenty thousand dollars for this party? If she was serious, then who did she think she was, speaking that way to an adult, and not only an adult but a religious leader (and potential customer) in the community? If she was serious, then somehow Middlestein had failed as a parent, and he was pretty sure he had not failed at anything in his life, even if he hadn't really succeeded at that much either.

After the meeting, in the parking lot, in the last car he had before this one (no, it was definitely not a Honda), barely after Robin had closed the door, she turned to give him one more smart-ass comment, and he greeted her with an open palm. Hard, he smacked her hard, he could admit it now. Maybe it was too hard. Maybe it was just hard enough. She pulled back flat against the car door and put her hands up to her face, and then she began to cry noisily. He started the car. He didn't care. Let her cry. And she did, the whole way home. He had thought hitting her would make him feel better, but it only fueled his anger; he could feel it clutching at his chest, a red-hot grip. "Cut it out, Robin," he said. She wailed and wailed.

When he pulled in to the driveway, she burst out of the car and into the house as if she were being chased, so dramatic as always. All he had done was hit her, his child, once, what was the big deal? Yet Middlestein felt his insides get sucked out and replaced with dread. His dad used to beat him with his belt, and Middlestein had done the same a few times (though definitely much less than his father) to his own children. Mostly he took his belt and bent it into a loop, snapping the insides together as a warning call. It had always worked; often the children would burst into tears just at the sight of it, never mind the snapping noise. But this was obviously different. This was less one part of an orderly system of punishment (bend over and take what's coming to you) and more an act of spontaneous violence. He had felt a jagged line of energy coming from his hand when he struck his daughter's face, as if a lightning bolt had sprung forth from it. Oh yes, for many reasons this was different, but perhaps the biggest one was that he hadn't discussed it with his wife first.

"What happened?" Edie, younger, thinner, but never thin, walking out of her office (always working, tireless, ceaseless, she loved her work more than him, this had always been obvious) and into the foyer, where Middlestein had stopped himself, helplessly.

"Our daughter . . ." Yes, that's smart, Middlestein, that's the tack, make sure she knows you're both in it together. "Decided to mouth off to the cantor."

"What did she say, exactly?"

"What didn't she say?"

"Do I need to go ask her what she said? Why is it difficult for you to answer the question? Why, Richard, is it always so difficult for you to answer the goddamn question?" Robin's crying stopped in a choke, regrouped, and then commenced even louder than before. Edie moved closer to him, and he found himself backing up flat against the front door. "Why do I have a child up there losing her mind?"

"She was completely disrespectful to the cantor," he said. He stood up straight. He was taller than Edie. He was her husband. He was allowed to make decisions.

"What did you do?" she said.

"I hit her," he said. "A slap."

Edie gave him a dark look—the pits of hell were in those eyes sometimes—and then burst out with her hands, her own lightning springing forth, slapping him on his shoulder, on his neck, on the side of his head, as far up as she could reach. "You don't hit my child," she said. Everywhere Richard covered himself, she struck somewhere else. "You are not allowed to hit her, do you understand me?" Her slaps stung him. Her lips shone with spit. "You don't go near my child." She hit him once more, in the face. "I have a deadline tomorrow and a terrified child tonight. It is like you don't want this house to function, Richard." She pushed a hand into his chest. "You are a ridiculous human being."

She shook her head and then ran up the stairs to her daughter's room, where, after a minute, the crying abruptly ceased.

Middlestein looked at Emily, smashed up against the window, dark, fearful eyes. She knew she had screwed up.

"If I were your father, I'd smack you so hard your head would spin," he said.

Emily's eyes widened, but she did not cry.

"But I'm not. I am your grandfather. So all I can tell you is that was just terrible, terrible behavior tonight. You, too, Josh. Just because you're the lesser of two evils, that doesn't mean you weren't being bad."

"I'm really sorry," said Josh.

"It's not your fault we didn't want to come," said Emily, remorseful at last. "I had a birthday party tonight. We both did. This kid at school."

"It was at a laser park," said Josh.

"I don't even know what a laser park is," said Middlestein.

"It's pretty cool," said Josh.

"I'm tired of going to the synagogue," said Emily. "We have Hebrew school all the time this year."

Middlestein let out an enormous sigh. "Emily, there are so many things we don't want to do in this life of ours. You have zero concept of this. You will someday miss this moment when the worst thing about your day is contemplating God's word for an hour or two."

"Doubtful," mumbled Emily, but he heard her, and his hand snapped out, and she jerked her neck back, and he nailed nothingness, just the air, the air between him and his granddaughter. He held his hand there for a second, and then patted her shoulder, as if that's what he had intended to do all along.

"You'll see," he said. "You'll see someday."

It was a silent car ride home; the children wisely kept their phones in their pockets, so it was just the sound of their breathing, the car engine, a light-rock station playing barely above mute. In their driveway they got out of the car before he had even turned off the engine and darted inside. Why were these children always running away from him? Didn't they know that he loved them with all his heart?

His son, Benny, walked outside, his arms tight across his chest, Rachelle only briefly poking her head out the door to wave hello, and then retreating inside, presumably to quiz the children on the night.

"How was it?" said Benny.

"The rabbi went on for way too long about Israel tonight," said Middlestein. "It's not that I don't agree, but he's like a broken record sometimes."

"The kids were okay?" said Benny.

"The kids were fine," said Richard. "I don't think they wanted to be there, but they're kids. They like hanging out with their friends."

"They kicked up a storm," said Benny. "There was this party—"

"I heard all about it," said Middlestein. "A laser park. Whatever that is."

"It's where they play with lasers," said Benny. He relaxed his arms. Middlestein had offered up just enough information to prove that he had bonded with the children. "There's one over in Wheeling. It's been around for a while."

Middlestein shrugged. "Whatever makes them happy, right?"

"Right. Well, they didn't get to go, so they weren't that happy about it."

"They're good kids," said Middlestein.

Benny nodded, looked back into the house, and then put his arm around his father. "You want to go out back for a little bit?" he said. The two of them walked around the front lawn, through the darkness, and onto the back patio, where Benny promptly pulled out a joint.

"You still doing that stuff?" said Middlestein.

"Once in a blue moon." Benny looked up in the sky. "It looks pretty blue to me tonight."

"I'd have a hit. Just one, though, because I have to drive."

"One's all you need anyway," said Benny. He lit up, dragged off it a few times, then a few more—*Blue moon my ass,* thought Middlestein—then handed it to his father. He immediately relaxed, the crush of tension in his heart and his back collapsing down toward the earth.

"Not bad stuff," said Middlestein.

"It's government grade," said Benny. "No hangover supposedly, though sometimes I'm a little slow in the morning." Benny sat down on a patio chair and motioned for Middlestein to join him. They both put their feet up on the table. Benny handed him the joint, and he took one quick last puff. "Enough for me," he said.

"All right, *no más,*" said Benny.

There was no crying upstairs, Middlestein noticed. Rachelle passed by a window, and then one light went out and then another.

"So. Dad," said Benny.

"Son," said Middlestein.

"I wanted to let you know something regarding the b'nai mitzvah," said Benny.

"So formal," said Middlestein, and he laughed. "What's wrong? I can still come, right?"

"Of course," said Benny. "I just wanted to give you advance warning about something." He stubbed out the joint and looked up and smiled weakly at his father. "Mom's got a boyfriend, and she's bringing him."

"How the fuck does your mother have a boyfriend?" *Who would want your mother?* was what he was thinking.

"Dad!" he said. "Don't talk that way about my mother, please."

"I just meant, already? That's all I meant. I mean, we only just split up."

"I don't know. She talked to Rachelle about it, and Robin's met him and said he's great, and Emily liked him a lot, too."

"*Emily* met him?" he said.

"I didn't have anything to do with it!" said Benny. "I can't watch over everyone all the time."

Middlestein shook his head. If he didn't have to drive, he would have smoked that entire joint right there, and it still wouldn't have been enough to calm him down. Some other man lying with Edie. He'd believe it when he saw it, and then he still wouldn't believe it.

"I wanted to let you know in advance so there were no surprises," said Benny. "I'm not on anybody's side but the kids'. We want them to have a good time and feel like they are loved by the family. And if it would make you feel better and you wanted to bring a friend, you absolutely could."

Beverly!

"I have to go," said Middlestein, who stood up awkwardly, knocking over the patio chair behind him.

"You don't want to stay? Rachelle cut up some fruit."

"I have a date," he said.

"Are you all right to drive?" said Benny.

"Never better," said Middlestein.

In the front seat of his car, not the old car, not the future car, just the car, his car that he had at this time in his life on this planet earth—crap, he was kind of stoned after all—he called Beverly on his cell phone.

"It's me," he said.

"I know who this is," she said. "It's a bit late to be calling." Oh Beverly, the sound of her voice slowly unfolding itself through the ear, luxurious, silky smooth, as he could only imagine her skin must feel like.

"It's not that late. Can I come over?"

Beverly laughed. "Well, I never expected to get one of these kinds of phone calls at my age."

"I just want to talk," said Middlestein.

"If you want to talk, we can meet somewhere," she said.

"Anywhere!" said Middlestein.

She paused, and he imagined her sweet breath flowing out of her mouth as loopy pink swirls of miniature flowers. "Meet me down at the pub, then," she said.

Through this town and the next one and the next—*Slow it down, Middlestein, the last thing you need is to be pulled over by a cop, try explaining that one to your daughter-in-law, you'll never see those kids again*—every last one of them looking identical to him. He was a part of this, his stores were, his store, the last one anyway, those other two closed (not failures, just not successes), but this last one, his legacy, the last one standing, he believed it was special. Was it not unique and important to have been one of the first Jewish business owners in the town? Had he not provided a service to his neighbors and friends? Was that not a success? Was he not worthy of being admired? Wasn't he worthy of Beverly's love?

Beverly, I'm coming for you.

The parking lot at the pub was nearly packed; it was the best fiddle night in the Chicagoland area, said the sign. He wormed his way through the lot, footsteps in gravel, dust rising in car headlights. The fiddlers fiddled. Middlestein straightened his suit coat, fluffed up his hair, his beautiful, thick, gray hair. Richard Middlestein, Jew, independent business owner, father, grandfather, a man—he believed—among men, walked into a dirty, crowded bar, where he had no business being on a Friday night, on a path to retrieve and secure the woman of his dreams.

He pushed through the crowd of middle-aged drunks knee-deep in Guinness and spilled popcorn and empty, crumpled-up bags of potato chips. They weren't even paying any attention to the fiddlers. Were they looking for love just like him? Where was it, where was love? What was it? Just what turned up in the dark?

Beverly, on a barstool at the corner of the bar, her hair in a ponytail, only a lick of makeup, dark mascara on those pretty peepers of hers. He must have called just when she was getting ready for bed. This is what she looked like right before she slept. For reasons unclear, he gave her a formal bow, and she laughed at him. He kissed her on the cheek, sat next to her, and took her hand in his.

"Enough waiting around, Beverly," he said.

"You're a married man, Richard," she said.

"Paperwork is being filed," he said. "I would say at this very moment, but the lawyer's got to sleep sometime." This was not entirely the truth, but it was close enough.

"That's not what I mean," she said. "All you do is talk about her all the time. I have listened to you talk for hours about your wife, your family, your grandchildren."

"But we talk about lots of things, Beverly! That's what I like about our relationship. So many interests."

"I have been down this road before. You are not available to me."

"I am so available. You have no idea," said Richard.

She shook her head, and her charming red ponytail swirled back and forth, and Richard lost himself momentarily in the sway.

"I'm serious about what I want from a partner in this life. When I walked into your pharmacy that day, it was because I'd heard from my manicurist there was a good, single man there."

"You knew who I was before you got there?"

"I'm fifty-eight years old," said Beverly. "I don't have time to waste."

"I find this flattering somehow."

"Don't let it get to your head. I was misled, obviously. You are so wrapped up in it you can't see your way out."

He was still holding her hand, and she was still letting him.

"I like you," she said, softening. "Don't think I don't."

The fiddlers announced that they were taking a break. They passed the hat, and the drunks began to dig into their pockets.

"We make good companions for each other," said Richard. "It would be so easy to take it to the next level. If you would let me be near you." He leaned in, close and desperate. "I'm trying to think out of the box here. Beverly." He kissed her lips, irresistible and soft, a young woman's lips; they were just what he imagined a young woman's lips would feel like. He thought of the ChapStick he saw in the bottom of her purse on the day he met her, forever softening her lips. "Beverly, Beverly, Beverly." He kissed her each time he said her name, until she was kissing him back, and the jolt to his groin was so furious he was afraid he might pass out in front of her. "I am a good man," he said. They kissed some more, and he heard her breathing turn funny, a breath unfamiliar and familiar at the same time. "I promise you." The intention was there. The intention was true.

Middlestein and Beverly, kissing and kissing until someone at the bar yelled, "Get a room." Middlestein and Beverly, taking their cars separately, a good fifteen miles above the speed limit, to Beverly's house the next town over. Middlestein and Beverly, crushing their hips and chests against each other on Beverly's overstuffed couch. Middlestein and Beverly, finally making their way upstairs, where they would push and pull and gasp and breathe and then wrap themselves around each other so perfectly and tightly to sleep that it was a wonder they had ever slept apart before. Middlestein and Beverly, two lonely people, successes, failures, a widow, a husband, caught up in something resembling love.

Seating Chart

THE MIDDLESTEIN B'NAI mitzvah, are you kidding me? We wouldn't have missed it for anything. They were our oldest friends in the world practically, or at least our oldest friends at the synagogue. We all came up together, Edie and Richard, the proud grandparents, and us, the Cohns, the Grodsteins, the Weinmans, and the Frankens. We attended each other's children's bar mitzvahs and their weddings, we have celebrated our birthdays together and anniversaries, too, plus sometimes Passover and the odd Thanksgiving, and every year, without fail, we have broken fast together. And now, to celebrate the first b'nai mitzvah of the third generation, was there any question we wouldn't be there? Who even knew we would live this long? There are no guarantees in this life.

The ladies among us bought new dresses at the Nordy's at Old Orchard and got mani/pedis from the Polish girls at the new nail salon where the Blockbuster used to be and blowouts from Lonnie, who we've been going to for years and don't know what we would do if he ever retired. The men got their suits dry-cleaned and gave up their tee times to a few of the new guys at the club who didn't know to call months in advance like they did. We all dieted a little bit the week before so we could eat whatever we wanted the night of the party. Some of us took our water pills even on days when we didn't need to.

We all sat together through the day and the night, first at shul, where we took our seats in the fourth row, the first row belonging to the Middlesteins: Edie and her escort, the Chinese man whose name we did not know; and Benny and Rachelle, the proud parents, with the twins, on one side. And on the other side sat proud Aunt Robin and her boyfriend, that charming schlub Daniel; Richard with his new girlfriend (also unmet, because no one ever introduced us to anyone), who sounded British from three rows away, which seemed impossible (though we later discovered was true); Rachelle's parents, straight as arrows, cool as cucumbers; and a handful of empty seats beside them, as if no one wanted to go anywhere near that traffic jam. The next two rows were filled with people we didn't know, but it was children mostly, and some out-of-towners we were guessing, and also we noticed Carly there— how could you miss Carly? So glamorous, even at sixty!—and some friends of Benny's and Rachelle's. We supposed we could have sat closer, fought our way through the out-of-towners, but we've sat in the front enough in our lives. Sometimes it's better just to sit in the back and watch. Watch, listen, and learn, that's what we say.

Little Emily and Josh sang their haftorahs beautifully, Josh's voice cracking during a high note, the whole room restraining their laughter, Emily a sullen, brunette, already bosomy beauty who smiled at nothing, and while we would like to think she was caught up in the majesty of the moment, it was more likely that she took after her grandmother Edie in her intensity. (We had all feared Edie at one time or another. The woman knew how to make a point.) Emily pounded away at her portion, as if she were adding exclamation marks where they did not need to exist. None of us knew what she was singing, but we all got the message: If she had not arrived somewhere yet, she was intending on getting there soon. Good luck with that kid, we all thought. She was going to be a handful.

We shared cars from shul to the party at the new (newish, anyway) Hilton. It had been built two years ago, and we had driven by it hundreds of times on the way to the health club, but why would we ever visit it? We already have homes, why would we sleep somewhere else? So we were excited when we got the invitations. Ooh, we said. The Hilton. We had heard good things through the grapevine. Plenty of bar mitzvahs and weddings had been held there, even if we were not invited to them, as we were at the age where we had almost been forgotten but were not quite old enough to be heralded for still being alive after all these years.

Of course we were seated together at the reception, the eight of us. We barely glanced at our place cards, which we picked up at the entrance to the ballroom from a table decorated with dance shoes: shiny black tap, pink satin ballet, bright red high-heeled flamencos, and a scuffed-up pair of Capezios. Flanking the table were two life-size photos on cardboard of Emily and Josh dressed in dance attire, and in the center was a sign that read, WE KNOW WE CAN DANCE. Charming, we said. Isn't that adorable? Some of us had seen the television show being referenced and watched it twice a week before bed, and some of us had better things to do with our time than sit around rotting our brains with garbage like that, especially when there were books to be read. Politely and calmly—some of us squeezing our spouses' hands for silence—we agreed to disagree.

The banquet room was just stunning, with a huge wall of windows facing a well-manicured rose garden backed by a trellis, the highway only faintly visible in the distance, and there was an atrium lit by strands of twinkling lights. Every table had a different dance theme and was decorated accordingly. Hip-hop! Broadway! Bollywood, salsa, and krump. (We never really understood krumping.) We were at Table 8—the waltz table. They must have run out of ideas for that, because all they had was two pairs of high heels on the table and a box of Viennese cookies. One of the husbands sat down first, opened the box of cookies, and offered it to the rest of us, but we all declined. *Not before dinner,* we demurred.

We were all silent for a moment. The table was covered with glittery stars and tea candles. The room was so romantic, but something was off. We were all thinking the same thing: Wouldn't everything be so perfect if there weren't two pairs of shoes in front of us? Shoes were just so unappetizing. Would anyone even know if we moved the shoes? Two of the wives exchanged glances, and then suddenly the shoes had disappeared, ditched under the table. We can't help it if we just want to make things a little bit nicer.

Around the room the other guests took their seats, and again we noticed the new configuration of the Middlesteins; the traditional notion of the head table was now kaput, with the kids sitting with their school friends, Rachelle and Benny sitting with Rachelle's parents and Edie, whose date had now disappeared, while at another table Robin sat glumly with her father, while her boyfriend chatted animatedly with the British woman, who seemed dazed, perhaps even a little angry, although she still held Richard's hand tightly. We wouldn't have wanted to be sitting anywhere else, but at the same time we wouldn't have minded being a fly, hovering back and forth between Edie and Richard.

We tried to decide if we should go over and say hello, but to which table? We had never officially taken sides in the split. We still saw Richard at the health club and said hello, we still spoke to Edie, who was no more erratic than usual, giving and taking her affection and attention from us; we loved her when we saw her, but we hadn't been able to count on her being emotionally present for years. Plenty of divorces had rolled through our lives, our children, our siblings, other peers, but we thought that once we hit a certain age, we were in it for life. When Richard left Edie after she got sick, *especially* after she got sick, there were too many ways to interpret it for us to decide how we felt. Everyone agreed that Edie was a tough woman to love, though she was worth loving. Was Richard saying that these unspoken rules did not apply to him? Was he a bold individual making a last grab for happiness? Or a coward who could not contend with fighting for his wife's life? Was he merely soulless?

Did we even know these two people at all?

We are happy to inform you we were not disappointed with the food. The salmon—obviously we all ordered the salmon over the chicken, because (a) we just knew that chicken was going to be covered in cream sauce, and boy, was it ever, and (b) you can't get enough omega-3 these days—was delicious. Also, the sauvignon blanc was so buttery it was practically sublime, and the women drank three glasses each, first depositing ice cubes from their water glass into their wineglass with their spoon, while the men, with the exception of the two designated drivers, drank Heinekens poured into glasses ceaselessly throughout the night.

At least a few of the Middlesteins had joined us in the celebration: Robin's head lolled gently on her boyfriend's shoulder, her eyelids barely open. We also were pretty sure we saw a bread roll go flying from the table where Edie sat over toward Richard's general direction, bouncing instead off his chair. Richard's girlfriend, who we had determined had a cute little figure on her and was at least five years younger than Richard, if not more, and who was overheard in the bathroom offering a stick of gum to someone, and definitely was British, or was at least British at some point in her life, *and* whom we never got to meet because we are apparently *unimportant,* made a not-quite-dramatic exit soon after this incident with barely a brush of lips to his cheek. We watched Edie watch this, and we watched Edie smile. Then she saw us watching her and hoisted herself up from her chair with the help of her son and came in our direction, walking slowly but surprisingly with ease, considering her weight, and, of course, those surgeries.

We had to admit she looked glorious, our Edie Middlestein, even as she was so ill of health. Her skin was a bluish putty, and she had gained another twenty pounds since the last time we saw her—was she three hundred pounds now? Three-fifty? We couldn't tell anymore—but her hair was dyed a deep, lustrous black color, and it sprang out beautifully from her head, and she was covered in a vibrant plum-purple caftan flecked with shimmering gold threads, and she wore a fantastic array of gold jewelry, the centerpiece of which was a long braided necklace from which dozens of charms dangled, bouncing up and down on her chest as she made her way toward us, until finally she was leaning casually above us. We could only presume she was channeling some sort of higher spiritual force (or dark demonic agent) to power her through the night.

"My dear friends," she said.

Dolly! we cried. We offered her our chairs, but she declined, instead grasping the back of Bobby Grodstein's.

"I'm sorry I didn't get over here sooner. There's just so much excitement tonight."

You look beautiful. How's the health?

"Enough about me. Can you believe the children?"

Could you be any prouder?

"Not possible."

But really, Edie, how are you feeling?

"Top of the world," she said, and she opened her arms wide, and then she stumbled a little bit, and Al Weinman, still so fit, jumped up and steadied her. "I'm fine," she said. "Too much excitement."

We said: Why don't you sit, Edie? What we were thinking was: *What a shame her husband isn't here to catch her.*

She did sit, finally, and we all unclenched whatever body parts we had been clenching. "The kids are going to do a little dance in a minute," she said. She did some jazz hands. "A little razzle-dazzle for the crowd. Hey, did you understand the theme?"

Yes, we're at the waltz table. It's a very old dance for very old people.

That cracked Edie up, and she laughed so loudly that other people turned and stared, but we loved that laugh, we loved her as much as she scared us sometimes. She was just so deeply feeling about so many ideas, and when she was present and capable of loving, she had astonished us with her fire. She had driven us to doctors' appointments and written us lovely notes when our children got married and brought deli trays over when we sat shiva for our parents. She had convinced us to try sushi for the first time, and also to donate money to Planned Parenthood, even though, obviously, none of us had ever had abortions. When she was engaged, she could make anything happen. When she was sad, and she had been so much lately, she could do nothing but eat.

We hid the shoes under the table, we whispered to her. Who wants to look at shoes while you eat?

Edie laughed even harder. "I'm glad you're here," she said. "My friends."

A smile so wide, the most charming cackle. It was hard to believe she had been killing herself for years.

The lights flashed a few times, and the conversation level in the room rose briefly, and then there were shushes, and then it was silent. Edie lifted herself up from her chair, blew us all kisses, and wandered crookedly back to her seat. In the corner near the DJ booth, we saw a stand with fourteen candles waiting to be lit, except it wasn't time for that yet, nor was it time for dessert, nor was it time for us to get our coats and head home, but the wine was hitting us, the Heineken, too. All we could do was sit and wait for Emily and Josh Middlestein to dance for their lives.

The lights went out for good, and then a *bomp bomp bomp* keyboard note started playing, and suddenly a spotlight kicked in on the dance floor—Christ, where did the spotlight come from? This Hilton had everything!—and out came Josh and Emily, both wearing little hooded sweatshirts, baggy jeans, and high-top shoes. The lyrics came on, that song we'd heard everywhere, those of us who watched television anyway and were still alive and kicking and trying to keep ourselves young. *I gotta feeling that tonight's gonna be a good night.* And then Josh and Emily danced! They pumped their arms, and they marched their legs up high, and then they crisscrossed them, and then they pumped their pelvises, almost all of it close to being in unison, and then they held each other's hands and did this jumping move, where their knees flew up in the air, and everyone burst into applause, Edie the loudest, whooping it up. And then when the singer sang "mazel tov"—followed by this strange electronic processed "*l'chaim!*"—the whole crowd shouted it at the same time, while Emily and Josh started this running-jumping action around the room, waving their arms to get the crowd up dancing with them, and everyone stood, the young people and the old people alike, and clapped along with Josh and Emily on their special day. We don't want to give too much credit to the song, because obviously it was the energy and enthusiasm of those children that got the room moving to the music, but we had to admit it was pretty catchy.

And then three video screens dropped from the ceiling simultaneously—would wonders never cease here at the Hilton?—and the opening credits of *So You Think You Can Dance* began to play, except, through the magic of technology, the title read, *So You Think You Can Hora*. Everyone got a good laugh out of that, but the laughter gave way to coos and awws, as a montage of baby pictures of Emily and Josh began to play, the two of them in incubators, so tiny, and then a shot of a young Rachelle and Benny (we had all forgotten it was a shotgun wedding of sorts) who were just twenty-one when they became parents. There was a giddy Aunt Robin raising a glass in tribute while holding Emily, the baby girl who had turned out more than a little bit like her, at least in attitude. And then both sets of the proud grandparents flickered on the screen, the crowd briefly quieting when a shot of Edie and Richard holding the infant twins appeared. Edie was still heavy then, but easily a hundred pounds lighter than she was now. Her face was so different: There was a person there to connect with, a jawline, a smile, a clarity in the eyes. No flesh hung from her cheeks and chin as it did now. She was in focus, we could see her, we could see who she was—or who we thought she was anyway. Where had that Edie gone? And where had Edie and Richard, our friends, our fifth couple, gone? We could not bring ourselves to look at her seated next to us. We did not want to imagine that our spouses could ever turn out like Edie, who had stopped caring about herself, or Richard, who had stopped caring about Edie. The room was suddenly frigid with a sickening mixture of heartbreak and mortality.

We waved our arms at the waiter. We begged for another round immediately. The room recovered, and we were treated to Emily and Josh in the bathtub, Emily and Josh on their first day of school, Emily as a ballerina, Josh in a tennis uniform, thirteen years of Halloween costumes, thirteen years of goofy faces, braces, ice-cream sundaes, summer vacations, chicken pox, school plays, the chubby period, the scrawny period, short hair and long, growing, growing, grown; thirteen years and still so many more to go. Oy, those *punims*. When the montage was complete, we burst into applause, poked at the corners of our eyes with the ends of our napkins. They weren't our grandchildren, but they might as well have been.

There was an intermission between the video and the candle-lighting ceremony, and we took the opportunity to drink. We skipped the ice, we drank straight from the bottle. We checked our watches, and thought about the errands we needed to run the next day, the walk we would take in the sunshine, the phone calls we would make to our children, some of whom lived in other states, with grandchildren we missed terribly. We had only been there for two hours, but it was already starting to feel late.

In our dreamlike state, we were unprepared for Carly's arrival at our table, famous Carly, who now worked in the White House and was friendly with Michelle Obama. (There was not a person in this room who was unaware of their relationship, thanks to a front-page picture in the Tribune months before the election, the two of them at a luncheon, tipping their glasses toward each other, a knowing grin shared between them; we had all stared at it on a Sunday morning, wondering what Carly had done so right and we had done so wrong.) Her skin was glowing and tight (too tight? tighter than our faces anyway), her blowout was impeccable, golden, tidy, and there was no question that her jewelry trumped all other jewels we had seen that night. We could barely look at her. We couldn't ignore her. She hovered over us and paused, waiting for a seat to be offered, a lifetime of offered seats trailing behind her.

"Ladies," she said. "And gentlemen."

Carly.

"We need to talk."

Do we?

"Are we not concerned about Edie? You see her all the time. Can you please fill me in on *what is going on here*."

With what?

"With her health! With her weight! You're her closest friends. How did she get to this point? And more important, what are we going to do about it?"

How did we tell Carly the truth? That watching Edie eat terrified us, so we had stopped dining with her. That her temper and will were impossible to fight. And that we had our own battles, cancer among us, one pacemaker, not to mention the usual trivialities: high cholesterol, high blood pressure, too-low blood pressure, iron deficiencies, calcium deficiencies, slipped disks, bad knees, gallstones, hormone-replacement therapy, on and on. There was nothing we could do for Edie that we did not already need to do for ourselves.

Talk to that husband of hers, we started to say, and then we stopped ourselves. Talk to Rachelle, we said. Talk to Benny. We're not in charge of Edie.

We finished our wine. Who did Carly think she was anyway? We raised our eyes to her one last time, her glittering anger.

But, we said. It is terrible, isn't it?

The candles were lit, various family members and friends traipsing up to the front of the room, but by then we had stopped paying attention. Dessert was served: cream puffs and éclairs on a tray. A chocolate fountain appeared in the distance. We were certain we couldn't take another bite of anything, but it would be rude not to sample the wares of the hardworking Hilton pastry chef. And those chocolate fountains didn't come cheap either. We ate and ate, and we looked at no one but ourselves until we were done.

Rachelle, who was lovely in a red silk dress with a sweetheart neckline and diamonds everywhere, clinging to her wrist, dangling from her neck, two big, bright studs planted firmly in her ears—*Nice try,* we thought, *but have you seen Carly?*—made her way to our table with a bright smile. No one had anything bad to say about Rachelle; she was just the kind of girl we would want our own son to marry, chatty, attractive, so slender, and put together. Mazel tov, we said. *Mazel, mazel.*

"It has been a wonderful day," she said. "Didn't the kids do a great job?"

They were perfection. But how are *you?*

She collapsed in an instant, leaning in close to us. "It's been a little bit hectic, as I'm sure you all understand. Some last-minute table changes. I was up until midnight redoing the place cards."

Things change before you know it. Don't blink twice.

"I did the best I could with where everyone sat. You're fine here, right?"

This is a lovely table, a lovely party. We couldn't have been more honored to be here.

She studied the table, doing some sort of math in her head.

"There were supposed to be some shoes here on the table. Were there shoes here when you sat down?"

We smiled steadily at her. We drained our glasses. We could not bring ourselves to answer her.

"There weren't any shoes?"

It's getting late, we said. The men helped the women up.

"There's going to be dancing in a minute," said Rachelle. "Stay for one dance."

We stayed for one dance. We box-stepped. We spun ourselves around. We were sweaty and drunk and we needed to go to bed. We clapped at the end of the song, and then we walked out the door brazenly and, we supposed, rudely. But if we didn't say good night, no one would even know we were gone. No one would ask, *Where did the Cohns and the Grodsteins and the Weinmans and the Frankens go?* And if anyone did, the reply would be simple: *I think they went home.*

We stood in the front of the Hilton and waited for the valet to bring our cars around. We held hands with our significant others. We stared straight ahead and ignored Edie and Richard, who had snuck out of the party and were standing nearby screaming at each other. We did not listen to what they were saying. We did not hear Edie say to him, "You do not get to apologize to me. You do not get that pleasure in your life. You do not get that reward. You are not absolved of one goddamn thing." And if we did hear her say that, we would not remember it the next time we saw her.

In the car, we were silent but for small belches and sighs and tears. We thought about our lives together, how we had risen and fallen and then risen together again, and then we went to our homes, and took our spouses in our arms, and we made love. And there was comfort in that, we were not cold, we were not alone, we had someone to hold on to in the night, our bodies were still warm, we were not *them,* and we were not dead yet.

Sprawl

KENNETH HAD REGRETS about the day. He had not wanted to leave his lady friend, Edie, behind at the party with her family; in particular, her estranged husband, Richard, about whom he had heard not one good thing. But Kenneth had a restaurant to run, and there was no one to take his place in the kitchen. Saturday nights were his best nights, second only to Sundays, when many people were lazy and without ambition and wanted someone else to cook their food for them. He had bills to pay. He had been behind on them for months. He had no choice but to go to work.

But first he had driven Edie from the synagogue to the Hilton in his twenty-year-old Lincoln Continental, walked her into the ballroom decorated with pictures of her grandchildren, the twins, Emily and Josh, who were celebrating their bar mitzvahs that day, and deposited her at her table, which was decorated with ballet shoes, a nod to a popular reality show about a dancing competition, which he had never seen because he had not owned a television set since 1989. He felt, briefly, as if he were checking her into a mental institution. When he kissed her good-bye, once on her cheek, and once on her lips, her son, Benny, who was seated next to her, threw himself into a noisy coughing fit. Kenneth squeezed Edie's hand tight and kissed the top of it. She was wearing a beautiful plum-colored dress that glittered. She smelled fantastic. She was overweight, and her breasts were tremendous. The night before, he had buried his hands and face and tongue in them, and was reborn in pleasure. *Cough away, son. I can kiss her all day.*

But that was a regret, too. He wanted her son to like him. He knew that Edie would still care for him even if her son didn't, but if Kenneth's own family was so important to him, how could it not be the same for this dear woman?

A final regret: that he hadn't walked up to Richard Middlestein and looked him straight in the eye and let him know what was what. A finger jab to the neck, he remembered that move from a long time ago. But it was not his battle to fight, it was Edie's, and he wouldn't think of getting in her way.

The minute he released her hand, he resolved to make it up to her.

Six hours later, after twenty tables had come and gone, Kenneth stood in the kitchen pulling noodles quietly, holding the dough high in the air and then twisting it, folding the dough in half, then stretching it again. The action was mindless, yet infused with love. He rolled the dough in flour. Long, thick noodles emerged, and as he twisted and halved and stretched, they quickly became shorter and thinner. Nearby sat cumin seeds, lamb, garlic, and chilies. These foods would warm her up. He had never met anyone with so much fire in her mind and heart as Edie, but with such a cold stomach.

She had allowed him to examine her tongue the night before, and it was pale and swollen. Her pulse was slow. He had put his hand underneath her shirt, and on her belly.

"Too cold," he had said.

"Come here, then," she had replied, her arms outstretched, her tongue lighting up the edges of her lips. "Warm me up."

His daughter, Anna, pushed her way through the double doors with the last of the dirty dishes. She blew back her purple-streaked bangs from her face and, as she bustled past, glanced at her father and at the food spread before him on the counter.

"Dinner for two?" she said.

He blushed. He was still thinking of all the ways he could heat Edie up. He had not felt this filled with desire since he was a young man and had first met Marie, his wife, now gone, hovering up in the sky somewhere. It had been eight years since she'd died, eight years since he'd had sex, and that time alone had felt cursed. Now here was Edie, reversing the curse.

"I could make some for you, too," he offered to Anna. He worried briefly that he had not been paying enough attention to his daughter while he'd been so busy becoming invested in this relationship with Edie. He saw her every day at the restaurant, though. They spoke all day long, even when they did not exchange a word.

Surely she was sick of this old man anyway. She had watched over him after their beloved Marie had passed away and he'd moved back to Chicago six years earlier, after failing at restaurant after restaurant across the Midwest. Once Marie and he had been ringers: Plant the two of them in a strip mall in any town and they could transform an empty restaurant into a successful enterprise, usually called the Golden Dragon, sometimes the Lotus Inn, and every once in a while New China Cuisine, which Kenneth disliked because he thought it had less character but Marie appreciated because of its efficiency.

They didn't pick the names; Marie's father did. He funded their start-up costs with his partners, and when they had built a solid base, he replaced them with less experienced chefs and sent them to the next location. They had left a trail of cities behind them: Cincinnati, Kansas City, Bloomington, Milwaukee, on and on, until Anna hit adolescence and begged them to pick a city and stay there. And so they picked Madison, where Kenneth was charmed by the pleasant academics who became their regulars and Marie admired the community's strong sense of responsibility to the environment. Kenneth did not like the cold winters or the drunken buffoons at the fraternities who harassed his deliverymen, but he had to admit that it was a pretty city, green and serene during the summers, and a nice place to raise a child. They lived there for five years, and then Anna went to art school in Chicago, and then Kenneth got the itch to move; he had enjoyed their life on the road. But Marie wanted to stay.

Kenneth said, "Is this it? Will we just live and die in Madison?"

Marie, fine-boned, clearheaded, not a fighter, said quietly, "There are worse places to spend the rest of your life."

"What about Cincinnati again?" he said. "Six months in Cincy. You liked it there."

She had not minded Cincinnati, it was true. There was a good bookstore there, and it was clean and safe, and they had enjoyed getting ice cream from Graeter's on Sunday nights, the three of them, Kenneth, Marie, and little Anna, the ice-cream cone almost as big as her head, it seemed. That had been fifteen years before, though.

"Why go back to where we have already been?" she said.

They moved to Louisville, where they had convinced Marie's father to open a restaurant in the Highlands neighborhood, on Baxter, where all the foot traffic was. They liked having a lively clientele. They bumped up their prices. They named it Song Cuisine, and they knocked down a wall and cleaned out a back room, and on the weekends local musicians came and played their guitars and sang. They were forty-five years old, and it was like they were twenty-two again, only they had never been twenty-two in the first place because they had always been working, and then they were parents and were already old. They had never had so much fun before. Anna came and stayed with them during winter break and said she didn't recognize them. "Who are you, and what have you done with my parents?" she said. Anna stayed out late one night drinking with a singer from Nashville passing through on his way to a show in New York City, and Kenneth found himself trusting his daughter like he had not before. He merely laughed when he heard her stumbling in late, cursing, and then shushing herself. The next morning he teased her about it. They were all growing into something new together. Madison was not it, but maybe Louisville was.

In a year Marie was dead from a cancer so rare there weren't even any experimental drugs to use, not that Kenneth would have wanted her to try them anyway. It was enough that she was going through chemotherapy. Marie had been born and raised in America. She believed in Western medicine because that was what she had always known. He thought otherwise, but he could not talk her out of it, so instead he tried to heal her with food. He cooked every meal for her day and night, using the herbs he had been raised to believe could heal her. Turmeric and red clover and ginger. When she no longer had an appetite, he brewed her tea with barbed skullcap. Anna took a semester off from art school and came to Kentucky to watch her mother die. They sat on either side of Marie and held her hands when she passed away. They were silent, and then they were sobbing. There was nothing left of Marie but a faded white shell of flesh.

Anna went back to art school, and Kenneth started moving again, but every restaurant he opened failed within months. Everything tasted funny to him. His father-in-law sent him a check and told him to retire. Kenneth moved to Chicago, where he found a basement apartment ten blocks from Anna in Wicker Park, with a small backyard. Stray cats used it as a thoroughfare, and he sat outside most days and watched them casually scuttle through fences and ivy. Even during the winter months, he sat there on a small stool he found in a scrap heap behind a Lutheran church down the block. Bundled up but secretly praying he might freeze to death. *This is where I will live and die,* he thought. The cats rarely acknowledged him. He often smoked long, thin foreign cigarettes. The tips of his fingers were cracked and yellow. He aged ten years in two. Gray hair, suddenly. Drawn cheeks, suddenly. Creaking bones in the morning, and no one there to moan to about it all.

At night he read poetry. That was how he had learned English years before: he had memorized American poems, so by the time he arrived from Xi'an to his uncle's home in Baltimore at the age of sixteen, he could speak the language and was both enamored and wary of his new homeland. He liked the Beats the best, the spunky revolutionaries, those who roamed their country in search of adventure. Ginsberg's "America" cracked him up.

He had recited the poem to Marie soon after they first met. His uncle was working for her father, an ambitious man who had immigrated from their same province as a teenager, and had built up his restaurant business with brutal efficiency. Kenneth was to work for him also; he came from a well-respected family of chefs. Marie was already working in the office after school. She was the one to hand him cash under the table. He asked her out for New Year's Eve, and they drank the terrible local beer, National Bohemian, at a party thrown by her cousin who was in nursing school. He whispered the poem in her ear, laughing when he said the line *When I go to Chinatown I get drunk and never get laid.* They were young, but she was not naïve, even if he was. Her slim hand resting on his arm, her eyes concerned, her lips amused. Or was it the other way around? *America this is quite serious.*

But thirty years later, in the basement in Chicago, he was memorizing poems for no one but himself. "America" suddenly felt dangerous to him. *Your machinery is too much for me.* He switched his attention to Robert Frost, wholesome and rural. But even he had a layer of darkness underneath his simple charms. He read a poem about an ant dying. *No one stands round to stare. It is nobody else's affair.* Lonely years sprawled out before Kenneth. He could have gone either way then. He could have died.

But Anna would not let him. Anna was watching over him, and she missed his cooking. Anna, who would not be denied a thing by her grandfather who could produce a truckload of cash in an instant, or at least enough to start up a new restaurant in a strip mall in the suburbs of Chicago. There was a bunch of paperwork, and in her eagerness to launch her father from his basement and out into the world, Anna might not have read everything she signed. The lawyer they hired was inexperienced, a friend of a friend who had just graduated from some law school Kenneth had never heard of in Indiana. They opened the restaurant, but the business side was a mess. Then it was just the two of them, father and daughter, sitting at a corner table with a stack of file folders in front of them at the end of a slow Tuesday dinner service, wondering what they had gotten themselves into.

The last customer of the night, a woman, a lush, vibrant, large woman, still remained, consuming the meal Kenneth had prepared for her with a fierce pleasure. She sucked on her fork and spoon and chopsticks, sipped in the flavors, his flavors, until all the food was gone. She had been there every night for the last two weeks. Kenneth liked her eyes; they were dark, and welling with anger. Her anger didn't scare him. He got it. He was pissed off too. His wife was dead. It had been a long time since it had happened, but the fact remained: His wife was dead. What was she pissed off about? Anna said something to him, demanding he return his attention to her. Her voice was husky, and her eyes were red, and while she had not cried yet, he feared her collapse. She was not to be blamed; she'd gone to art school, not business school. Marie had always handled the paperwork; she had grown up working the books for her father. What did either of them know? How could Marie have left them behind like that?

And then the woman rose from her table, the last customer, this late-night goddess, heaving, licking the last of his food from her fingertips, and came to their side. She said, "Maybe I can help." She had been a lawyer once, a long time ago, but not so long that she had forgotten what she knew. "I was very good at what I did," said

Edie Middlestein. She said it like it was a promise.

She sat down next to Kenneth and Anna and smoothed the papers with her hands. She squinted, and then she was appalled on their behalf, and then she laughed at all the little loopholes that danced before her on the page. "This," she said, "can be fixed." It would take a bit of work, but she could make it all better for them. "I've got nothing but time these days," she said.

He wiped the flour from his hand and onto a towel. The finished noodles rested nearby. Kenneth threw the cumin seeds into a skillet. He thought about adding cinnamon to the dish. If cumin would be good for Edie's health—he knew she was sick, even if she wouldn't tell him the truth; her skin was too pale, her breath too slow—the cinnamon would be good for her passion.

It took only two minutes to roast the seeds. The chilies were chopped, the garlic, too. The crunch of the cumin would be a nice contrast to the tenderness of the lamb, and he knew that Edie would enjoy it, the texture, the depth, the surprise of the pop. He mused on the cinnamon some more. How would Edie feel if she knew he was adding an aphrodisiac to her food? He decided all he would be doing was adding a little flame to an already burning fire.

His cell phone rang, and he answered it, knowing that it could only be Edie, because she was the only person who ever called him at night besides his daughter. In fact, she was the only friend he had.

"Darling," he said. "Did you behave yourself?"

He emptied the roasted cumin into a small bowl.

"I did not," she said. "I might have thrown something at my ex-husband's head."

Kenneth chuckled. "What did you throw?"

"I don't know. It was all a blur. A roll, I think."

"Did you hit him?"

"No, it bounced off the top of his chair, and then it landed on the table in front of him."

Kenneth laughed harder.

"Why do I do these things?" She sighed into the phone. "I don't even care about him. I care about you."

"Someday you will stop being angry with him," said Kenneth.

"But why should I care what he's doing if I'm crazy about you?"

"We are allowed to have more than one feeling at once," said Kenneth. "We are human beings, not ants." Sometimes he ached for Marie, but he would never tell Edie that. He was glad she was nothing like Marie, in physique or personality, or he might have ended up comparing the two of them. The only thing they shared was their head for business. All he knew about was cumin and cinnamon.

"I have a thousand feelings at once," she said.

"That's a lot of feelings," he said. "You must be a strong woman, then."

"Or crazy," she said.

"Fine line," he said.

"Razor thin," she said.

"I am making you something special," he said. "But I must ask you something first."

"Ask me anything," she said, and he knew she was not lying.

"I was going to put some cinnamon in your food, and sometimes it works to . . ." He lowered his voice to a whisper. "It's supposed to turn you on."

"Oh," said Edie.

"Do you think that's cheating?" he said. "Maybe I shouldn't need the cinnamon. Maybe I should be enough."

"The more cinnamon the better," she said. And then, urgently, she said, "Use a lot of it."

"I'll be over within the hour," he said.

"Hurry," she said.

What was left to do? He put on a pot of water for the noodles. He tossed the lamb with the cumin and chili and garlic. A teaspoon of cinnamon. Soy sauce. Some salt and black pepper. There was a grind in his groin; more cinnamon. He poured some oil into a pan, and heated it, then added the lamb. A pinch of salt on top of that. The noodles in the boiling water. He hadn't had any fun in so long. He hadn't cared about anything. A minute later the lamb had gone from cherry red to brown. A few cumin seeds popped. He pictured a small butter roll flying across that hotel ballroom and landing on the table in front of her ex-husband, and all his earlier regrets merged into just one: that he had not been there to see that happen.

His daughter, his beautiful daughter with her vibrant clothes and her sticklike legs and her boots that made her look as if she were heading off to war, stomped into the kitchen with the last of the dirty dishes from the night. How had such an original human being come from the likes of him? And she was faithful to him. His faithful child.

"You hungry?" he said.

"I don't know," she said. "I think I'm mostly tired."

He was relieved. He did not feel that it was appropriate to give the food he had made for his lover to his daughter. No cinnamon for his baby girl. His heart swelled suddenly toward Anna, as if someone had struck him in the chest. He was bruised with love. He came out from behind the stove, and then embraced his daughter. Her small bones beneath him. She was not Marie. She was something else.

"Did I say thank you?" he said. "Did I say thank you for saving my life?"

She started to cry. "Not out loud," she said.

"Thank you, thank you, thank you," he said.

When they finally pulled apart, her face was

lightly smudged with purple streaks. She ran the tips of her index fingers underneath her eyes.

"You're killing me, Dad," she said.

He rubbed her shoulder, kissed her forehead.

"No more then," he said.

He sent her home. He emptied the pot of noodles into the strainer. He tossed the noodles and the lamb together and spooned the finished dish into a carryout container. He loaded the dishwasher. He took off his chef's coat. He washed his hands and face and lifted his shirt and washed under his arms, too. He was tired. He slapped his cheeks. Edie Middlestein awaited.

He drove through one town to the next to the next. Every mall looked the same from a distance, but he had spent enough time in them—his whole adult life—to know that they were all unique, even if it just came down to the people who worked there. Busy little American ants.

Every house on Edie's street was dark except for hers. Was it that late? He checked his watch. It was after eleven, and he was meeting his lover. He was a young man again. Once, before they were married, Marie and he had driven to Atlantic City on a whim, and they had arrived after midnight and stayed up till dawn gambling and kissing. They got dizzy from cigarettes. That evening, he had a second wind and a third wind and a fourth wind. But tonight he would settle for a second wind.

The front door was unlocked, and he entered, calling her name, but she did not respond. The light was on in the living room, where they had first kissed, lavishly, luxuriously, for hours. They had embraced each other on the couch in front of the window that faced the street. Anyone walking by the house could have seen them. It did not feel dangerous to do it, but it did feel prideful, which had its own kind of danger. *Before destruction,* he remembered. He had memorized parts of that book, too, just to see why so many people were interested in it.

There were framed pictures of her family everywhere, but not a one of her husband. She had taken them down. There were empty squares on the wall. Which was worse? To leave them up, or to have the gaps left behind as reminders of what once was?

He went to the kitchen because he knew that was where she would be. Already eating before he even arrived with dinner. Eating all that junk food she craved, the cookies and chips and crackers, giant tins and boxes and bags of crap. That was what was making her sick. Eating things made by machines rather than by hand. He was going to change that, if he had to cook her every meal himself.

In the kitchen the freezer door was open. Inside it sat an open pint of ice cream, a spoon still sticking out of the top. He looked down, and there was Edie, sprawled on the floor in her shimmering purple dress, one hand outstretched, the other frozen near her chest, as if she had clutched at it, and then given up on it. Her lips were blue. This was not right. This was the wrong information. He knelt beside her and put a hand on her face, and the cool skin rippled beneath his fingers.

He grasped desperately for another poem he had memorized once, the exact lines of which eluded him. It had something to do with an icebox and plums and being sorry for eating them, even though the person speaking in the poem was clearly not sorry at all. It had always felt like a joke to him. The funny poems were usually the ones he remembered. It still felt like a joke now. It read like a note you would leave someone on the kitchen table when you were walking out the door and never coming back.

His eyes blurred with tears, and then there was only a haze of Edie. He was a fool to think he could have love twice in this life. Arrogance. He held her hand to his chest with both of his hands. No one was entitled to anything in this life, not the least of all love.

Middlestein in Mourning

RICHARD MIDDLESTEIN WAS uncomfortable in his suit. It had been five years since he had worn it, five years since he had been to a funeral. There had been a string of them in 2005: his mother's, his father's, his Aunt Ellie's, a second cousin named Boris he didn't know particularly well but who lived nearby in Highland Park so he went as a representative of his side of the family (by then he was the only one left), one of his estranged wife Edie's co-workers' (a suicide, terrible), Rabbi Schumann (they had to rent some tents for that one, so many people came), and at least three more that he couldn't recall at that exact moment because he could barely breathe. He hadn't gained more than a few pounds since then, but his flesh lay differently on his body now. Gravity had struck, and skin gathered around his waist, creating a small buttress of fat between his ailing chest and still youthful legs. He hadn't noticed it till he pulled up the zipper on the pants. He'd had to suck in his gut. He'd been holding it in for hours now.

To make matters worse, he couldn't stop eating. There was food on every surface of his son's house, the living-room table, the kitchen table, the dining room table, a few card tables that had been dragged inside from their garage, the glass end tables on either side of the living-room couch. And the food kept coming, friends of Edie's—friends of theirs, he supposed, when they had once been together—streaming through the front door, all holding different offerings, kugels and casseroles covered in aluminum foil, fruit salads in vast Tupperware containers, pastries in elegant cardboard boxes tied with thin, curled ribbons. His oldest friends from the synagogue, the Cohns and the Grodsteins and the Weinmans and the Frankens, had all gone in together on the elaborate smoked-fish trays. He had heard them mention it more than once that day, but only when someone wondered out loud where the delicious fish had been purchased, and one of them offered up the information. "We went this morning right when they opened," they said. "It's the least we could do."

Middlestein would have thrown in a few bills, too, if they had only called him, but they had not. No one had called him about anything at all, not even to extend condolences, except for his son to give him the details about the funeral. But why would they? Why had he thought anyone would care how he felt? He had left her, and they had been weeks away from signing divorce papers. He put his plate down on the floor and lowered his head between his legs and let it hang there. He had brought two boxes of rugelach, and he realized when he walked through the door that it was not enough. Nine months before, he would not have been allowed to bring a thing. Nine months before, shiva would have been held at the house they shared together. Why didn't he bring more rugelach? How much rugelach would he have had to buy to not feel this way? How much rugelach would he have to eat?

He jerked his head up. He wasn't certain he was feeling rational. He was so full, but still he wanted more. All around him, people sat politely with plastic plates in their laps. His son, Benny, sat on a low chair, his granddaughter, Emily, leaning against her father, staring off into the distance, her lips downturned. She was thirteen; it was her first funeral. Middlestein's daughter, Robin, sat next to Benny on a normal-size chair; she was working hard at actively not looking at Richard. Her boyfriend, Danny, sat next to her. He held her hand. He was stroking it. He had these fancy-framed glasses, but he wore his tie loosely, like he'd never learned how to tie it on his own. He looked like a real pushover, is what he looked like to Richard. *That's about Robin's speed,* he thought. She'd need someone to mow right over.

Robin was hell-bent on ignoring most of the traditions, but she at least wore a black ribbon pinned to her blazer. She wore one, Benny wore one, Rachelle wore one, Emily wore one, and so did her twin brother, Josh, who had wandered off somewhere toward the dessert table. Richard was not wearing one. Richard was not sitting on a low chair. He was on the couch, with the rest of the general population. He had sat in the third row at the synagogue during the services. He didn't know if that was too close or too far. He didn't know if he should have leaned against the back wall, like some of the other mourners. It was standing room only. Good for Edie, he thought. People still cared about her. People wanted to show their respect. When he died—oh God, he was going to *die someday*—he wasn't sure he'd get the same kind of crowd. Not anymore.

He was suddenly consumed with a desire for savory foods, the saltier the better. He wanted his tongue to be swollen with salt. He hefted himself up from the couch—What was that sharp crunch in his knee? And the other in his lower back. Had those always been there, or were they brand-new?—and maneuvered through the crowd made up of people he had once been able to pat on the back hello and who now pulled away from him, he was certain, in disgust. He made his way to the dining room table, to the herring. He was going to eat the hell out of that creamed herring. He spooned some onto his plate. He grabbed a handful of baby rye crackers, and then he stood there and dipped one crisp cracker after another into the tangy, smoky whitefish. He could stand here all day, if necessary. At least he had something to do, a purpose for standing in that spot, at that moment. It was then he thought he understood Edie, and why she ate like she had; constantly, ceaselessly, with no regard for taste or content. As he stood there, alone, in a room full of people who would rather take the side of a woman who was dead than acknowledge his existence, he believed he at last had a glimmer of an understanding of why she had eaten herself into the grave. Because food was a wonderful place to hide.

In the living room, his daughter death-stared him. Her eyes were sloppy with anger. It was spilling out everywhere. What a mess. Danny stood behind her and gripped her shoulders, and Robin reached back and pried his hands away from her. Danny winced. *I'd happily walk her down the aisle just to get rid of her,* thought Richard. *Hand her off to that guy in a heartbeat.* Robin got up from her chair, and again the crowd cleared a path for her, and again people stared. She marched up to Richard and past him— leaving behind only the slightest trail of a sneer— and toward the kitchen, where she paused and then dramatically shoved open the swinging door that separated it from the living room. Richard could see his daughter-in-law, Rachelle, inside, a cup of coffee in her hands, leaning against the refrigerator. Rachelle was the captain of this ship, and Robin was a rebellious sailor. Mutiny was clearly afoot. "We *have* to talk," was the last thing he heard before the swinging door settled to a close.

Richard turned his attention to the circular dessert table, where Josh was opening boxes of pastries and shifting them onto a giant vaseline-glass dish that Richard recognized as one of his aunt's. She had brought it with her from Germany when she immigrated and left it to him when she died, along with a houseful of furniture, which he had since sold or donated to charity. But he had kept the dish. It was made of uranium, and it was light green and glowed faintly like kryptonite. It was a neat trick: The dish was made of a volatile substance, but had been turned into something useful. As a child in Queens, he had been mesmerized by it. He would fantasize about it exploding spontaneously. *Poof!* The Middlesteins would be gone forever.

A week earlier that dish had been sitting in Richard's former living-room cabinet, and now, suddenly, it was on his son's dining room table. He bet that his house had been ransacked. Rachelle had probably gone through every cabinet and drawer and taken whatever she liked, antiques, jewelry, those two fur coats. Now he was going to have to have a conversation with his son about it. That was his plate, everything in that house was his, lock, stock, and barrel. No papers had been signed, nothing had been filed. If Edie had lived a bit longer, it's possible he would have had no say on that plate whatsoever. But she hadn't. Edie was dead.

Josh had opened the last pastry box and was arranging a small assortment of chocolate-dipped cookies around the edge of the dish. When he finished, he moved the dish directly into the center of the table, and then took a step away, examined the table, and smiled. Middlestein glanced over, and then looked back: Josh had arranged the cookies on the plate in the shape of a smiley face.

"Josh!" he said.

"What?" said Josh.

"You can't do that." He pointed at the plate. "That's not appropriate," he said. Thirteen years old, and no common sense. Had he had common sense at that age? Can that even be taught?

"I thought it would cheer people up," said Josh. "Everyone's so sad."

"Aren't you sad?" said Middlestein.

"I don't know what I am," said Josh.

"Well, you should be sad," he said. "It's a terrible thing that happened, your grandmother dying."

"You think I don't know that?" said Josh. 5-4-3-2-1, and he was in tears. Then he ran out of the living room, and upstairs, and everyone in the room stared at Middlestein, and if he wasn't already the most horrible person in the room, this sealed the deal.

In the kitchen, Robin was confirming it with that mouth she had inherited from her mother: loud, big, bossy, and self-righteous. He walked to the swinging door and leaned against the wall next to it, listening to her yell.

"You don't know anything," she was saying to Rachelle.

"They were married for nearly forty years," said Rachelle. "You don't know what that's like."

"I see. So you're superior to me because you're married and I'm not."

"That's not what I'm saying, Robin."

"She *hated* him. Don't you understand that?"

They were arguing about the rights of the living versus the dead. It was true, his wife had hated him, not just after he had left her but before then, too. Yet he had hoped in this small way that eventually, after they had divorced and everything had settled down, he with his new girlfriend Beverly, her with that Chinese man she had been dating recently (who had just arrived, and was now standing in the corner of the living room with his purple-haired daughter, the both of them stunned and silent), after they all had rearranged themselves into new formations, that he and Edie would be able to come back together as friends.

He had told no one this wish before, and he wasn't even sure if he deserved her friendship, but they had created these people, Benny and Robin, and they, in turn, had created lives for themselves, and he and Edie shared those two beautiful grandchildren (even if Josh was oversensitive and Emily a little mean), and he had imagined that one day they would watch them graduate from high school, and college, and dance together at one or both of their weddings, that they would be able to sit next to each other, share the same air, laugh about things that had happened a long time ago that only they knew about, secrets just for the two of them and no one else. He had left her because she was killing herself and killing him, too. And now he was saved: He had fallen in love with a woman named Beverly, and she had fallen in love with him, too. Now he was more alive than ever, and he had wanted Edie to have the same experience, but it had been too late for her. Too late for love. And now he was the only one who knew their past. He was the only one who knew that eventually, one day, Edie would have forgiven him. He had been there with her the day her father died and held her hand and stroked her hair and taken her into his family and life when she had no one left, when she felt she was an orphan. One day he would have reminded her of this. One day she would have been in his life again.

"He didn't kill her," said Rachelle.

"He might as well have," said Robin.

Upstairs, loud music began to play, a song that

was played at Josh and Emily's b'nai mitzvah just a few days before. The mourners looked even more stricken, their skin colorless, their lips grim. Music was incorrect. Benny left the room casually, but as soon as he hit the stairs, he raced up them.

"I'm an orphan now!" screeched Robin, but her words blurred within the bass of the dance music.

She's going to regret saying that, thought Middlestein. *Someday she'll want her father again.*

But she does not regret it, at least not while he's still alive. (At his funeral, however, she is devastated. She heaves tears, Daniel's arms locked around her shoulders, the other family members distant from her, battling their own grief.) She barely speaks to him for the next decade, and then only briefly, at family functions. Sometimes they only lock eyes across the room, and then she'll look away, her lips crumbling with hurt, but still he treasures those moments. She ignores him at Edie's unveiling ceremony, and at Emily's and Josh's birthday parties and graduation ceremonies, and even at Benny and Rachelle's twentieth-anniversary party. She doesn't invite him to her wedding. He only hears about it a few months after the fact, and it is an accident that it is even revealed to him. At Benny's house he sees a picture of Robin in her wedding dress standing with bridesmaid Emily. Beverly is there with him—by then she is his wife—and she looks so devastated on his behalf that he can't help but sob for a moment, and he has to excuse himself to the restroom, and he stays in there too long, his hands clutched to the sink counter, leaning forward, missing Edie, missing his daughter, wondering if what he had done wrong was really that terrible, and wasn't life full of layers and nuances, colored all kinds of shades of gray, and the way you felt about something when you were twenty or thirty or forty was not how you would feel about something when you were fifty or sixty or seventy—he was nearly seventy!—and if only he could explain to her that regret can come at any time in your life, when you least expect it, and then you are stuck with it forever. If he could do it all over, if he could have that one shot, he would have fought harder for his life with Edie, he would have fought harder for her life. No, that wasn't true either, because there was a knock at the bathroom door: Beverly, checking up on him, gently holding his hand, his second chance, his late-in-life angel, her skin still smooth everywhere but around her eyes, her figure, her smile, her hold on him, on his heart, on his flesh. There she was. This was why he had traded one life for another.

But he was not there yet: He had only begun to regret; he had only begun to understand; he had only begun to mourn. Middlestein's daughter was fighting with his daughter-in-law, his son was walking downstairs and then into the living room, shaking his head angrily, and his dead wife's new boyfriend was now sobbing on his son's living-room couch, his hands clutching his kneecaps, his daughter's arms wrapped around his chest. The music upstairs stopped.

"She wouldn't have wanted him here," said Robin. "I can speak for her. I am totally correct in speaking for my mother."

"He has every right to be here," said Rachelle, and he could tell then that she was done discussing the matter. It was her home, after all. No one could argue with that. It was the woman's home. It was her show.

Robin slammed the kitchen door open and burst into the room. The mourners turned their heads away. Don't look at the poor girl. She's lost her mother. Robin left through the front door, but moments later appeared in the backyard. Everyone could see her through the window, sitting on a deck chair near the pool. Benny appeared next to her. He pulled a joint out of his pocket and lit it. The two of them got up and turned their deck chairs facing away from the house, and passed the joint back and forth.

Middlestein was still leaning against the wall near the kitchen, unable to move. Rachelle pushed open the swinging door and poked her head into the dining room, holding her gaze on Middlestein.

"I'm sorry," she said.

"What do you have to be sorry about?" he said. "You didn't do anything."

"The yelling," she said. She shrugged her tiny shoulders. She did not seem tough enough to take on his daughter, but he understood she would do anything to keep things under control in her universe. Other days she would not consider Robin and her tantrums and her ego. Rachelle might have been a princess, but Robin was the little sister. Today, though, Rachelle had restored order, at least in small part on Middlestein's behalf. He would never forget that she did that.

She looked, bleary-eyed, at the tables of food before her. "What are we going to do with all this food?" she said.

"It'll get eaten," said Middlestein. He tried to muster up a joke about Jews and food, Jews and funerals, Jews and Jews, but nothing was funny.

Rachelle wandered past all the tables and then did a double take in front of the dessert tray that Josh had decorated to look like a smiley face. She turned back to Middlestein with a sour look on her face, cheeks pinched, forehead wrinkled.

"Wasn't me," said Middlestein.

She began to push all the cookies together in a big pile in the middle of the plate, and then she knocked some off, then finally she picked up the plate, weaving her way through the crowd, out the front door, until there she was, standing near the pool, handing cookies to her husband and her sister-in-law. She took one for herself and picked at it with her fingertips, one tiny bit at a time. She paused and licked her lips. In another minute Robin's boyfriend, Danny, showed up by her side. He dragged up a seat for himself and Rachelle. Together, they all hid.

What was left for Middlestein in this house? Everyone he cared about had run away from him and all the other mourners. He should leave. He had paid his respects. Whatever was left for him to feel was for him to experience alone. And he wanted to take his suit off. He wanted to burn this suit. He pushed his way through the crowd, nodding at anyone willing to give him eye contact. He paused at the front door and considered following his children to the backyard to say good-bye. He decided against it. Out front, outside, it was sunny, and he felt warm and tight in his skin. He couldn't breathe. Middlestein unbuttoned his pants and hunched over. He heard a small choking sound and lifted his head up. By the oak tree, near the mailbox, there was his granddaughter, Emily, crying. He pulled himself up and walked toward her. Sometimes she got this calm look on her face, and that's when she looked like Benny. When she was dressed up, she looked like her mother. When she was angry, she was Robin, she was Edie. When she was clever and funny, she was like them, too. *When does she look like me?* There she was, alone by a tree, weeping for her grandmother. He wanted to weep, too. He went to his granddaughter and he hugged her and held her against him, and just like that, they were close. Until the day he died, they were close. Wasn't that strange? No one would have put the two of them together like that. No one would have figured they had much in common except being family. But they were close to the end.

Acknowledgments

Irving Cutler's thorough and fascinating book, *The Jews of Chicago: From Shtetl to Suburb*, was tremendously helpful during my research. I am grateful to Dr. Benjamin Lerner, who was always so thoughtful and generous in his explanations of vascular surgery, as well as the health issues of overweight Americans. Lisa Ng gave me a spirited education on Chinese cooking; if not for her, I would never have known about the magical powers of cumin and cinnamon.

Kate Christensen is the best first reader a girl could have. Deep talks with Wendy McClure were invaluable to the development of this book. Rosie Schaap, Stefan Block, and Maura Johnston have all provided love, support, and couches on which to crash. My agent, Doug Stewart, has probably achieved saint status by now. And my editor, Helen Atsma, is a powerhouse, as well as a very nice woman. Finally, I would like to extend a big thank-you to WORD Brooklyn, my favorite bookstore in the world.

About the Author

Jami Attenberg is the author of *Instant Love*, *The Kept Man*, and *The Melting Season*. She has written for the *New York Times*, *Salon*, and numerous other publications. She lives in Brooklyn, New York, and is originally from Buffalo Grove, Illinois. Visit her online at jamiattenberg.com.

Center Point Large Print
600 Brooks Road / PO Box 1
Thorndike ME 04986-0001 USA

(207) 568-3717

US & Canada:
1 800 929-9108
www.centerpointlargeprint.com